THE SHIPS

THE SHIPS

ROBERTO QUESADA

Translated by Hardie St. Martin

Four Walls Eight Windows
New York • London

A Four Walls Eight Windows First Edition
Copyright © 1992 Roberto Quesada López
The original Spanish-language edition of *los barcos* was published in 1988
by Baktun Editorial, Tegucigalpa, Honduras.
English translation copyright © 1992 by Four Walls Eight Windows.

First Printing April 1992
All Rights Reserved

Library of Congress Cataloging-in-Publication Data:
Quesada, Roberto, 1962–
[Barcos. English]
The ships/Roberto Quesada;
translated [from the Spanish] by Hardie St. Martin
p.   cm.
ISBN O-941423-65-4: $17.95
I. Title
PQ7509.2.Q44B3713   1992
863—dc20   92-7988
CIP

FOUR WALLS EIGHT WINDOWS
P.O. Box 548
Village Station
New York, NY 10014

Jacket and book design by Martin Moskof.
Printed in the U.S.A.

For my mother
who was never able to read me;
her glasses arrived when her life
was about to leave her.

For my brothers and sisters:
Ana, Norma, Lisandro, José Adán,
Eduardo, María, Iván, Marta,
Fernando, Hugo Saúl. For four
million Hondurans.

And for José Adán Castelar
compañero and poet.

. . . and out of these waters come ships to destroy them to wage a dirty war on them a war of hunger a war of misery a war of desperation and daily terror a war that lays waste destroys burns kills maims a war of the powerful who possess ships and guns versus the barefoot and hungry and naked who have learned much from the dreams handed down from generation to generation by their grandfathers. And the grandsons who became fathers and grandfathers. . .

—Manlio Argueta
From *Cuzcatlán Where the Southern Sea Beats*

What's wrong with me? I'm old but not crazy and what I'm looking at is a spirit. Yes, the spirit of a dead man; yes, that's it, because you don't exist, you're nothing, you're just a blotch, a blob, something false and transparent trying to scare me. You knocked on my door a minute ago. Nobody's ever knocked on my door—nobody—because nobody knows about it, except my dog, but my dog no longer barks, doesn't scratch at the door, won't ever make a sound again. He's dead and what's dead can't make a sound, like you, watching me with the long silence of the dead. But your eyes are deceiving, they seem to be alive, and that's something. Nobody can come this far, and what's more, nobody would want to, because there's no reason why they would find anybody living here. You can't talk because you have no voice—like everything that has no life; it was my imagination, yes, my crazy old head that made me imagine your voice when I opened the door; my frazzled brain made up the voice that said 'good afternoon, grandpa.' But it's a voice without a body, and a voice without a body is no use at all.

You won't stop looking at me, kind of happy and scared at the same time, the way my dog would watch me when it was cold and shivered like a noisy run-down engine. You won't take your eyes off my face and I feel like glass. Clean, shiny glass without any smudges; that's what I am in your eyes—the glass window in a store displaying God only knows what, maybe my soul. And I'm not afraid of anything but your look upsets me, gets me all mixed up, and I think maybe you're real after all, flesh and blood like me, because spirits wear white, but not you, you're dressed like a young man who's come from far away. Your face reminds me of somebody I can't place, but it looks familiar. Maybe I knew you in the other life they talk about . . . But what silly things run through my head! I'm old but not the least bit stupid. The rooster crowing frightened you, ah you poor scared kid, if you had to live like I've lived, alone in this corner of the mountain, alone all these years, maybe since before you were born . . . and I never scare, not when a rooster crows anyway. Come in, kid.

1

"That woman's driving me crazy, Chon."

The old man folded the tortilla and, bringing it up to his mouth, said:

"Those women are not for the likes of us."

It was Guillermo's fourth day at work and sheer chance had brought him and her together. It wasn't that Guillermo was such a skirt-chaser or loved to exaggerate, but as he put it to Chon, the woman had embraced him with her eyes.

"And do you know her name?"

The old man made a wry face that said: forget the damn woman.

"Instead of thinking about her, you ought to be asking me things you don't understand about this job; maybe then you can stay on here."

Guillermo pretended to forget the woman and listened—nodding—to: "Look you can't act dumb here. There've been poor fucking slobs they let go on working a whole month without gloves. And they've got to produce or else they get sacked. So what happens? After they've grabbed hold of enough pineapples, their whole hand gets cut to a bloody pulp. Or they get allergies from the pesticides and some even end up with TB from the sun and rain. And the minute the bosses see them looking sick, they fire them. You can't be stupid around here, because the stupid guy gets fucked. Move along and make like you're working hard, but don't kill yourself, because it's not worth killing yourself around here."

The old man got to his feet:

"It's noon, time to get back on the job."

"This lunch hour is over fast, we should have at least two hours."

"Yes, but as far as they're concerned it would be better if we didn't eat lunch. Look at me, I've been working at this for years, and d'you think there's any breaks for me? No, us older guys have to work as hard as the young ones. A worker's a worker wherever he goes."

They both went into the field:

"Right now there's lots of pineapples, so if you're interested in getting overtime money you have to get a move on. The Captain has to see you putting in a lot of work."

He thought of the plantation as if it didn't exist, as if it were a legend or fiction. He, a city boy, working like all the other farmhands. He had to learn to get the city out of him, live with them, catch on to their talk, their habits. About the farmhands he knew only what he'd heard, but he had a hunch he'd learn to get along with them, that they'd like him because he'd try to do his best. He was sure of it, maybe because he was scared of what people said about them: that they'd just as soon kill you as not if you looked at them the wrong way. Or maybe because his people came from there, from the country. He wasn't sorry that his work was here in the hot sun, so far from the city, since there were no openings in the city anyway. And if something did come up, it was for a gardener or for help in the supermarket where they paid next to nothing, less than what you needed to eat. So in the end the plantation was the only salvation for those lucky enough to land a job there.

While he was cutting pineapples and dumping them into the enormous sack slung over his back, he remembered, after they told him he had a job on this plantation, how proud he had felt whenever anyone asked him *Where do you work?* And how he thought he should act differently, like he was somebody when he answered *For the Standard Fruit Company*. It was now four days since last Monday, the day he had started, and he was now used to being wide awake by 3 a.m.; oversleeping would mean he'd lose his job. On that morning four days ago, he walked toward the bus stop into a world that was new to him. With everybody around him, talking about the things they'd done on Sunday, he took a liking to a toothless man because he'd break in after every third word with a *What a sunuvabitch* and Guillermo found that funny.

All of a sudden everybody was shouting *Here comes the tin-can, here's the kidney buster!,* and the bus came into view and pulled to a stop, its horn making a lot of racket, and everybody trying to squeeze into the small space inside. Guillermo felt an arm on his shoulder, prodding him, *Look alive, kid, or you'll get left behind,* and it was old Chon, whom he didn't know yet. In the bus he couldn't make himself comfortable; he was thinking of the thirty kilometers they'd have to cover to get there, and he couldn't imagine what his job would be like. He noticed some of the guys sleeping and others talking. To break the ice, *It's hot in here, isn't it?* he said to the one next to him and the man looked startled: *Hot?*

"What are you thinking so much about?" old Chon shouted over at him.

Guillermo smiled:

"About my first day of work, the day you shook me up to get me into the bus."

"The thing is, if you fall asleep you're out of luck and if I hadn't warned you, you probably wouldn't 've got here. Tomorrow's already Friday, pay day. I've done pretty good because I put in a few extra hours, and that's something anyway."

"Are you going to La Ceiba this Sunday?"

"No, no, I don't go very often; last Sunday it was because I went to the Stadium. I almost always go when the Olympia team comes, but that little trip hurts my pocket too much. Last Sunday I missed the bus and couldn't get one till Monday morning. Well, you saw me."

"I'd like to see the town where you live."

"Good, that's no problem. I'll take you there. But I want you to know now, so you won't say later I didn't tell you, there isn't much to see in El Porvenir."

"I'd like to see it, old man Chon."

Guillermo's shoulder ached. He wasn't used to the weight of the black sack that could hold so many pineapples of all sizes. You went up and down the lanes, filling it to the top and then carried it to the small street where a truck waited to receive all the fruit we had cut.

"This is some fucking sun, Chon."

"Hah, you get your ass soaked twice here: from the heat there is all morning and because it rains almost every afternoon. There's no way to get out of it."

And, as a matter of fact, a huge black cloud was starting to take shape at the foot of the mountain. Guillermo watched it:

"You're right, Chon, it's going to rain."

"You mustn't mind it; it's not the first or the last rain."

"My mother says it's bad to get wet after being in the sun such a long time. She says it gives you TB."

6

"That's nothing," he said and started telling Guillermo stories that made his flesh creep.

He told him that once a fellow worker had eaten a pineapple, had gotten terrible stomach pains right away and half an hour later he was dead:

"And we buried him right here," he said and couldn't keep from smiling.

Guillermo already knew some stories from the others who worked there, like the one about all the *barba amarilla* (yellowbeard) snakes in the area. *A snake that looks at you and hypnotizes you,* a fellow near him had said, *Your feet take you to it, it bites you and you live only another three minutes.*

"Chon, there are no yellowbeards around here, right?"

"Whew, kid, there's plenty of 'em! Right now you may be standing on one and don't even know it."

He jumped, drawing a belly laugh from the old man:

"No, yellowbeards only come out where there's a lot of bush. Around here, only one or two come out from time to time."

Rain started pouring down. The workers hurriedly unfolded pieces of plastic to cover themselves. Guillermo, who carried nothing to shield him from the rain, thought about falling sick.

"That's how fucking bad it is around here," Chon, who was covered with a small piece of plastic, shouted, "you got to find something to keep from getting drenched."

"What? The rain doesn't let me hear good."

"Oh nothing," the old man said, holding his hands to his mouth to form a horn, "just that you're going to die of a fever today."

Guillermo, who wasn't used to the way the workers kidded among themselves, took literally most of what they said to him and he believed it was true that he wouldn't live past this day. He could already hear the radio saying *We deeply regret to report that today the young man known as Guillermo López López in this life delivered his soul to his Divine Redeemer; a wake will be held at . . . Guillermo López López has passed on; eternal peace be in his soul and Christian resignation for his family . . .* He could imagine people drinking coffee, his family weeping, and the girl he had discovered that morning crying disconsolately, dressed in black, sobbing *I loved him, he was the one I'd always dreamed about . . .*

Chon's shout pulled him back to reality:

"How come you're so quiet?"

"Oh I was just thinking."

"Don't tell me you were thinking about the woman you talked to me about this morning."

"No, no, I'd already forgotten her. And, speaking of the woman, d'you know her name?"

The rain was coming down harder:

"No, kid, nobody knows the names of those women who work in the Office, not even God; they think they're Tarzan's mother and aren't even near as good as Chita."

He thought the old man might be right, more than likely so, but not about this one; after all, Chon hadn't been there to see the way she kept looking at him. When they had called him in to sign his work contract that morning, she'd been there, and he had noticed that there were other secretaries too and not one of them, not even the one taking care of him, had looked at him; she was the only one who had stopped writing in her corner and stared at him for a long while. He could swear that she would have talked to him, if he hadn't gotten so nervous, but he didn't want to say this to Chon—since all he could expect for an answer would be *Cut the horseshit, kid,*—but he had seen her smile at him.

Aha, yes, I believe it's around here. It must be there in that hut. I feel nervous and it's no joke walking all by myself through this tangled shrubbery. If Chago was along it'd change things, because he knows the bush. But who knows where you are now, Chago. People leave and you never hear from them again. The hut looks deserted; there isn't a sound; anyhow I'm going to knock. No response, nothing, nobody. But this has to be the one because there isn't any other. I hear something . . . looks like the door's opening. Good afternoon, grandpa. What's the matter? Well, aren't you my grandfather?

Why is he so quiet? He must've gone deaf or else doesn't understand the way people talk anymore. Mom said he came here a long time ago, and I wondered why he came to live all alone so far away? I don't know; his eyes scare me; maybe I made a mistake. It looks like he's trying to say something but can't; in this place with nobody to talk to, anybody can lose his tongue; but why does he keep on staring at me like I'm some kind of freak?

Maybe he doesn't recognize me; it must be that; mom told me that I was very small when he left home. He liked me a lot and used to take me wherever he went; he wanted to bring me here but she wouldn't let him. What would have happened to me if she had? Well, that's all in the past and, besides, he never brought me. I wish he'd let me in so I could rest awhile; my legs are shaking; I don't think I've ever walked so much in one day. But there's always a first time in this life. I can't take my eyes off his; they look like mom's when thinking to herself about something. It's almost dark and grandpa doesn't ask me to come in. Maybe he's deaf and dumb.

I'm going to use sign language to see if you can understand me. I feel silly; it's as if his eyes were accusing me of not making sense. What can I do? I can't go now. Even if he's not my grandpa I've got to find a way to get through to him and ask him to let me stay the night. I'm not budging from here and nobody's going to make me; how can he think I'm going to wander around alone in this jungle in the middle of the night? No, I don't know how I'm going to do it, but this man has to recognize me. Look at me closely and think. I'm Guillermo, Guillermito, cute little Memito, agoo. What crazy things are running through my head? And who knows what I look like. Grandpa must be right not to remember me. It's late and he seems ready to spend the whole night staring me in the face. How creepy! Sunuvabitchin' rooster! I'm making such a big fool of myself, every little thing makes me jump; it's a good thing I got scared though, otherwise you wouldn't be smiling at me now, grandpa. What did you say? To come in? Is it really true or am I dreaming? Yes, yes, thanks, now I'm the one who's deaf.

2

Pay time came around. Everybody was happy. The Captain in charge of the crew passed out the pay chits. Guillermo felt as if he owned the world: it was the first time he had so much money. He looked the chit over: *López López Guillermo. Total amount. Received and approved.* They got into the cart that would take them to headquarters where they had the crating machines, the commissary, and the general offices—right to where the woman was who had embraced him with her eyes.

They arrived; the noisy crowd was in a festive mood. Chon showed him the ropes: *You have to get in line and wait for the paymaster to show up. We'll meet afterward down by the commissary.*

He stood in line with the hundreds of workers who waited —shouting, whistling, pushing—for the moment when the magic chit was converted into paper money.

Fascinated, surprised, Guillermo had never been caught up in the middle of so much laughter and shouting, *C'mon, stop pushing, don't forget to pay me back, Manuelito,* and the car with the loudspeaker going full blast with the Mexican ranchera song, *How many times now they've thrown me out of the Tenampa*. He'd have preferred something else, maybe one of those he heard on foreign radio stations at midnight like *It's your perfume, woman, that always turns me on;* but no, the car's loudspeakers knew only Mexican songs. He thought maybe it was because those were the songs that people liked. The guy behind him was almost busting his eardrums, singing along with the loudspeaker, *I carved your name into the cactus leaves.*

The shouting grew louder. He figured that the paymaster was in sight.

"I finally got my pay. That line is terrible. How'd you manage to get paid?"

Chon smiled and nodded: "You got to be on your toes around here, kid. You don't want to stand in line? Look, did you notice that there are two soldiers outside the pay booth? Well, you walk over to them and say you'll give them something if they let you pass. After you get your pay, slip them a *peso,* and that way you don't have to fart around with the line. See how easy it is? That's why I'm always one of the first to get paid. Ah! one thing: don't try to put one over on them or they'll fuck you up. They've done it to a lot of guys who tried to play smart; give them a *lempira* and you've got it made."

The commissary was jam-packed; Chon, who always seemed to be one up on everybody else, had no trouble getting served so that, he and Guillermo soon sat on the edge of the sidewalk with fresh drinks to talk.

A man more or less Chon's age came over to them. Chon greeted him with much deference and immediately introduced Guillermo. The man said his name was Luis but everyone called him Luyi; he sat down between them and asked where they were going next.

"The kid wants to know El Porvenir so I think that's where we're going."

12

Guillermo asked Luyi where he lived and he answered, *Not too far, in a place called Bonito, pretty, except that there's nothing pretty about it; anyhow, I can show it to you one of these days.*

"We have two kilometers to walk," Chon said.

"That's no problem," Guillermo answered, "there's about five from where the bus drops us off to come to work."

"Not too bad," Luyi added.

The first thing they found at the entrance to El Porvenir was the cemetery. Guillermo thought about the things he could say about a cemetery in a short story or a novel; maybe look into the life of each person buried there and tell his or her story. Right away the idea seemed tacky to him. What important person could possibly have died in El Porvenir? He didn't know why the hopes that had been hidden away for a long time came back to him now; he walked along thinking of the interesting things there must be in this town to write a good book about. All of a sudden a phrase came to mind; he didn't know its source but he hadn't forgotten the words: *Describe your hometown well and you will be a universal writer.* Now he felt he had his own variation: *Describe El Porvenir well and you will be a universal writer.* From then on he jotted down, on imaginary paper in his brain, everything he saw and that this was a sad little town: dirt and cobbled streets, people looking out through doors and windows to see who's going by whenever they hear the sound of shoes knocking on the cobblestones, old men who all look alike, humble, sad, or anxious, empty trees, without fruit or leaves, trees that appeared to be trying to kill themselves.

"What's the matter, thinking about that woman again?"

"No, Chon, I was thinking about something else."

"There's always something to think about," Luyi chipped in.

13

The three trudged along as if they were climbing up a steep hill.

Luyi with his head down, Chon saying goodbye to hands that appeared in doors and windows.

"How do you recognize them if they don't show their faces? And why don't they show their faces?"

"That's something not even I know. I noticed it when I first came to live here and as time went on I got used to greeting people from my house like that too, just sticking out my hand."

He cheered up. Describing a town where only hands greeted you from windows and doors seemed fantastic to him. Who'd ever dream up something like that? Not even great writers. He thought maybe he was now old enough to start noting everything down, with the remote idea of writing it in a book some day. It was hard because he knew there were universities in the capital where they studied literature; he had barely finished high school and his economic situation made him forget about getting that far. Chon and Luyi were walking along so deep in thought that they didn't hear Guillermo's laugh. He remembered that when he was a small boy people used to tell him that since he liked to write the best thing for him was to go to the capital to study letters. Back then he had imagined himself holding a scalpel in his hand operating on an M, cleaning cavities in a capital Z, putting a cast on the leg of a lowercase z that had probably broken it playing soccer. In his childish innocence he had believed that when he grew up he'd have a lot of letters and nobody would mess around with him, because the first one to try it would suffer the consequences of an F in the face or a J in the chest and children would be afraid of him because he would punish them with a Y or with the vowels.

"What are you laughing at?" Chon asked.

Breaking up, he threatened:

"You want me to use a K on you."

"What's that?" they both asked together.

Guillermo explained and the three laughed, walking easier, as if they had come to the top of a hill.

Small, built of bamboo and wood, Chon's house was near the beach. His wife looked like a good model he could use to round out his description of El Porvenir: greasy apron, hair unkempt, like a hairdo mussed up by the wind, two missing front teeth and that way of laughing as if to keep from showing them. All this along with other details made him decide that the woman would be a character in his future books, maybe a character that would only show up now and then but would be very important because she was a faithful portrait of the woman of El Porvenir.

She served coffee. Chon and Luyi were talking about the sea; fishing wasn't so good these days. Guillermo didn't join the conversation. He was observing the children, thinking that all El Porvenir kids must be no different from Chon's kids, who were playing on the floor, building castles with matchboxes, making roads that took them from one structure to another on tiny wooden cars put together by their father: honking horns, outwitting the police who were trying to take away their license, making trains and boats that sailed on seas drawn on the floor, bringing down their airplanes on the enormous landing field the whole house covered. Chon's wife came over to explain that she was letting them play because it was the weekend; they didn't have to go to school and had already done their other chores this morning: taking water out of the well, fetching firewood, running errands, feeding the chickens, and the like.

"Do you want to see the grounds?" Chon offered.

Luyi stopped at each plant, carefully checked each stem, its leaves, asked how many months had gone by since they had been planted, and murmured, as if to himself: *Yessir this yucca is the best kind,* and the same went for the avocado, *Yessir this is the best kind of avocado,* and the same with the peppers and everything else Chon had planted.

"You sure know how to tell the best," Guillermo said half seriously.

Luyi smiled, running his hands through his gray hair.

"It's just a bad habit I've picked up," he answered, smiling.

"It would be nice to go take a walk around town," Chon suggested to Luyi, "so this kid can get a look at some of it even if, like I told him, there isn't much to see here."

"*Wanna go wichyou papa,*" Chon mimicked his son. "They want to go everywhere; no, you're staying right here, this is only for big people."

The center of town held the soccer field, and around it the more important spots: the town hall on one side, the church on the other, across from the town hall a bar and across from the church the Juan Ramón Molina School.

"They ought to fix up this field," Guillermo said, running his eyes over the pot holes in the paths people had made crossing the grass from one side to the other.

"The mayor doesn't want to; if it was up to him, he'd get rid of the field altogether, but he's left it here so as not to have any trouble with the people."

Looking a little puzzled, Guillermo asked:

"Doesn't the mayor like soccer? It's unusual for a mayor not to."

"Yes, sure, he likes it. The thing is, Town Hall's in front of one of the goals. One day there was a game on, the El Porvenir team against one from Tela. The visiting team scored a terrific goal against the local team, the damn ball flew in through one of the Town Hall's windows and, to make things worse, smashed right into the mayor's face."

Guillermo and Luyi laughed:

"And what happened then?"

"Well, the mayor came out with the ball under his armpit, wiping blood off his face with a handkerchief, pulled his pistol out right there and fired a bullet into the ball; and that was the end of that game. Next day the Mayor's Office published a law banning soccer on week days and they only play on Sundays since then."

"It's the least they could do," Guillermo said with a big smile.

Luyi was watching two cows go onto the soccer field and, talking to himself, said:

"Simon Bolivar was born in Maracas . . ."

Guillermo broke in:

"No, that's not it, it's Simon Bolivar was born in a cattle ranch in Caracas with seven cows, one very fat and one very skinny, and all the others loaded with ticks."

"Skinny and loaded with ticks, yes," Chon said, "but there isn't even one fat one here."

Luyi suggested that they go into the bar and the others agreed. Inside, the place was busy. Chon explained that on Saturdays people started coming in from first thing in the morning, so what could you expect by 3:00 p.m. The bar was quite big and wasn't completely full. They found a place near the juke box.

"I don't like beer much," Luyi said, "but since you're going to have beer, I'll have the same."

The waitress came over and it was Guillermo who ordered for all of them. Luyi got some change to play music.

"With this kind of heat beers go down like they came from heaven," Luyi said as he sat down.

"You mean there's beer in Heaven?" Guillermo asked.

"Maybe, you can never tell."

"Don't joke about holy things," Chon warned.

"Don't get so serious on me," Guillermo answered him. "Beer's something very natural and they may sure enough have it in heaven. And it'd be a good thing if they did, because then a lot of people would be good just to get in."

Luyi laughed. Chon didn't know if he should get mad or not. Guillermo imagined St. Peter in an apron, with a pistol in his belt, asking, *"what'll you have?"* and shouting for the benefit of those who couldn't read the big poster hanging on the wall that it was strictly forbidden to spit on the floor, or discuss politics, or religion.

"Are you thinking of that woman again? That's really something."

"No, Chon, if you only knew what I was thinking about!"

"Should I order three more?" Luyi asked.

The waitress came back. Guillermo's eyes were lost in her low neckline and when she turned around he gawked at her short skirt and her well-rounded legs.

"That's for young guys," Chon observed.

Luyi looked as if he disagreed:

"Well, if you watch carefully that's not right. Wait till she comes back and take a good look, it's not just the young she leads on."

"You said it," Guillermo added, clapping his hands, "Chon hasn't noticed."

Three more beers arrived; on the juke box one of the songs Luyi had marked was playing, *These shoes I'm wearing are all torn,* and Chon:

"Well, go buy yourself another pair, Luyi."

At that moment the waitress went by and six eyes zeroed in on her back. Chon said something like you guys were right and Luyi's song said *I've got it bad, I get it coming and going.* Guillermo raised his hand, showing three fingers, and the waitress signaled that she'd be right over.

"What time is it?" Chon wanted to know.

"Seven; no, eight . . . I mean quarter to seven," Guillermo answered.

"You can't go back to La Ceiba now," Luyi said, "no buses at this hour."

"Yes, yes there is," Chon spoke up, "a bus leaves at ten on Saturday nights."

"Then we can have another," Guillermo said.

"Sure," Luyi answered, "and another and another till it's almost ten o'clock."

When the waitress came back Guillermo asked her to have a soda or anything she liked with them, and she said okay she'd be right back.

"These beers have hit me," Chon murmured.

"I can still stand a few more," Luyi said, as if to himself.

"No, no, no; that's not what I mean. I can stick around till daylight," Chon protested.

After waiting a long time, the other song Luyi had selected finally came up and the waitress sat down next to Guillermo who was singing along with the juke box *Life ain't worth a thing, liiife ain't worth a thiiing,* and Luyi joining in with *Always starts out cryyying and ends cryyying too* and Chon joining in, *That's why in this wooorld liiife ain't worth a thiiing.* Guillermo, under cover of their singing, stuck his hand under the table to feel up Lili. That's the name he thought she had given him. Taken up with their show, Lili wasn't objecting and he made the most of it to explore deeper, to where he could feel it getting warm.

Three beers later, they were all pretty high. Lili stood up to go the bathroom. Chon asked:

"Are you thinking of going to bed with that woman?"

"No, she's working, feeling her up is enough for me."

"You're a devil," Luyi said with a laugh.

Lili came back.

"I think we're leaving," Guillermo said.

"Okay, fine," she answered, "let's go to some other place."

Guillermo was surprised:

"Aren't you working?"

"No, I'm off at eight. I've finished my shift, otherwise I couldn't 've sat down with you."

Chon had a tremendous desire to laugh and this was further increased by the look on Luyi's face, who was feeling the same thing; they couldn't stop themselves and filled the bar with their explosive laughter.

"What are they laughing at?" Lili asked.

"Don't mind them, they're drunk."

His grandfather's laughter flooded the air. Guillermo was smiling, happy to be the cause of what was making the old man double over. Everything seemed suddenly different in the cabin.

"What time do you go to bed, grandpa?"

"I don't have a set hour, I sleep when I'm sleepy," his grandfather answered, still smiling.

The old man got up and offered him coffee. As pleased as he was to have a visitor, he was even more pleased that it was a relative he adored, even if he'd had a hard time recognizing him at first. Not until Guillermo mentioned names, places, and events, ones they both knew, was his grandfather able to pull it all together.

"This coffee is delicious."

"I planted it with my own hand."

"No wonder."

His grandfather sat down again and, after thinking for a few seconds:

"What is La Ceiba like now?"

He was in trouble now. He could do many things but he couldn't describe places; he hadn't managed it in previous tries, not even when he had started to write a story about the pineapple plantation or when he tried it with El Porvenir, and what disheartened him most was the conclusion he had come to recently, on his own: describe El Porvenir well and you'll be a universal writer. Faced with his grandfather's questioning look, he thought of the first letter Chago had sent him:

```
Dear Guillermo:

    How are things going, dude? I hope
you're having fun. Me? I sure as hell am,
everything's fucking great. Things are cool
here, smooth. Excuse me for not writing be-
fore this but you know how it is, you're
in for it when you come here like a dumbo
who's not with it but I'm falling into
stride. Let me tell you something, this so-
called Tegucigalpa's nothing out of this
world like they try to make you swallow
when you don't know it. No, life here drags
on like an old turtle. The city is all ups
and downs like a roller coaster. And the
first days the cold used to scare the shit
out of me, but I'm used to it now. We just
finished the first semester and I was sen-
sational, a real champ, didn't flunk a sin-
gle course; and I'm not going to La Ceiba,
```

because I'm hard up for bread. Besides,
during vacation they have what they call
summer courses and I'm going to sign up because the sooner I finish, the better off
I'll be. I live away from the center of
town, but not too far; in the Kennedy resi-
dential area, that's a little like La
Ceiba. There are big dance parties every
weekend but they're nothing like the ones
we used to have. Anyway, I go to them every
now and then so as not to forget how to
shake the old skeleton.

I've gotten to know some places or, better yet, all of Tegucigalpa. I'll take you
when you come. Get this, I went to Belen, a
neighborhood with more whorehouses than you
can shake your stick at, and they have everything from fairies to very beautiful
hookers, well-stacked, firm young things.
But it's not worth going there. They say it
used to be but not now; .since the marines
came all kinds of diseases have popped up.
Something called AIDS and the Flower of
Vietnam are the most common. They say if
you catch them your dick rots off. What do
you think of that? Everything's been fucked
up. I also went to El Picacho. It's a very `
tall hill from where you can see the whole
city and all the houses look like matchboxes, the cars like ants and the people like

the little dots on computer screens. Down-
town is like La Ceiba: the cathedral, the
park, the disco, the banks and so on, except that there's a Promenade here, a street
for pedestrians only. I don't dig this
Promenading bit much, but you ought to come
and see it. There'd be a lot of stuff for
you because girls sixteen years old and up
cruise around on the Promenade. Most of
them walk like they're just showing off
their butts and the guys are all a big
front, wearing fruity sweaters and that
sorta thing.

I'm having a great time. I'm shackin' up
with an American girl I met at a rally, who's
spending a few months here. She's pretty and
besides she has an ass that, well, you can
imagine what it's like. And besides, she
helps me keep body and soul together. She
always slips me dollars when I run short. Of
course I also have a girlfriend, a hundred
percent Honduran. We've got to consume the
native product. If I didn't keep a cool head
I'd be half in love. But no, my means of support comes first and the best way for that is
fucking the Americans. Well, as I was telling
you, my girlfriend lives close to where I
live, she's more stubborn than a mule, lets
me feel up everything and I've taken down her
panties twice, but the minute she sees I mean

business, she starts calling me names, pulls it back up and scoots off. One of these days she's bound to fall.

About what you said for me to look into, I'm doing it but it's hard getting to know writers around here. But don't worry, I've got a friend who also likes to write and he's going to put me in contact with writers; once I'm in touch with them, I'll mail you their addresses so you can send them your stuff.

By the way, I miss La Ceiba and sometimes at night I think about everything there, weekends with everybody in bathing trunks and swimsuits for the beach, dances in the evening at Brillo del Mar, Centroamericano, Disco, El Patio, Lido—in fact, the whole great scene, like in the Crazy Horse disco. Yeah, La Ceiba is a different set up; for instance, going off to La Isla neighborhood at night to look for girls and afterwards to the big dance shed the blacks run, to have fun with those cats. D'you know, a few days ago I dreamed that I was walking down by the pier, in the Barrio Inglés and that the hookers there were all like movie stars, very goodlooking and friendly... is that right? Shit no, that neighborhood won't ever change; those whores are quicker with a knife than anybody from Olancho. The best thing about the Barrio Inglés neighborhood are the baleadas. People around here don't know what a baleada is; I sound like a parakeet repeating myself: it's a very popular dish in La Ceiba, a flour tortilla topped with black beans and cheese. And people here say, So those are the famous baleadas? And I say to myself, some day they'll have a chance to eat them and they'll lick their fingers. Here they have a lousy popular saying that goes: While Tegucigalpa thinks, San Pedro Sula works and La Ceiba has fun, and then I answer I'd rather have fun then spend my time thinking shit or working for the gringos. So what do you say Guillermo? I'm real sure you think I'm right. Some people ask me what La Ceiba's like and I get into a big thing because how can I tell them everything it is? I start out with the streets, how wide they are and lined with palm trees, not like here where instead of streets they have alleys. And I tell them there are more blacks than pebbles and when they ask me why so many blacks live there I tell them the joke: the blacks live near the beach because Columbus told them he was coming back for them and they're still waiting for him! Did you know that one? I can say it because I'm black. It's a long

time since I last went swimming because the
only river here is the Rio Grande, but the
grande part about it is a lot of bull. It
looks like a mud hole, the water comes up
to your knees and it's filthier than the
mouth of a girl I happen to know at the
university. And you won't believe this: the
river runs right through the middle of town
and divides Tegucigalpa from Comayagüela.
I'd like you to write to me soon and if
possible also send me some postcards, one
with the beaches, another of the center of
town with San Isidro Avenue in it, and the
park and Town Hall. And send me another of
the estero (inlet). About the estero, here
they ask me what it is and I've got to use
my wits to explain it; I tell them it's a
kind of river but not quite, that it splits
La Ceiba in two, that is, the part with the
beach and the other where the center of
town is; I looked for that little word in a
dictionary and I'm not convinced, because
for us the estero is something else, it's a
tourist attraction.

I guess I've tired you out by now, making
you read all this crap because that's the way
it is, because there are some things you're
committed to do, like reading my letters. I
hope your novel won't be like that (I'm joking); I've got a hunch it's going to be among

the best. Speaking of your novel, keep this
letter, when you write the novel maybe this
will help you some; but, one thing, correct
all my mistakes and don't put them in to make
it look original, otherwise what will my
friends think? Another thing, I haven't told
anybody our secret about your novel. And I
want to ask you a favor: If you use me as a
character its OK, go ahead, but with the name
I go by in La Ceiba, "Chago," but don't forget to mention my complete name, Santiago
Reyes del Olivo as well, at least once. I'd
be very grateful for that.

When you write me back tell me if you're
still going with Idalia, if don Lelo's gone
to Haiti, all about Chon, Luyi, Fabian, and
your other new buddies. Say hello and tell
them I know all about them and that one of
these days they'll each get a letter.

Well, Guillermo, regards to your family
and tell Idalia to stick with you; you're a
good man. For you a strong hug. See you
soon.

Chago

His grandfather smiled. It had worked; thinking of
Chago's letter had helped him describe the place so the
old man would understand.

"People and places change so much!" said his
grandfather, nodding his head up and down.

"Wasn't La Ceiba like that before?"

"No, my boy," he said with a knowing air. "I'll tell you what it was like, but first go on with the rest; you've told me almost nothing about this kid called Chago."

He smiled, pleased that his grandfather should show such interest:

"Yeah, sure, but let's take one thing at a time, grandpa."

3

I didn't know what the commotion was all about. The workers were milling around and somewhere a loudspeaker was blaring.

"Things are going to get nasty," Chon warned.

"Why?"

"Don't you see, Guillermo? They refuse to give the raise and the Union wants us to go on strike. But they say if there's a strike the Company'll go away, and if it does, where's our food to come from? Strikes are dangerous; during one of them the Company can up and leave and it's goodbye La Ceiba. Everybody in La Ceiba will get fucked; all the people there work for Standard Fruit. These strikes scare me. Look, a few years back we went on strike here for the same thing, so they'd give us a raise, but the Company didn't want to. And since all us workers have to stay here till it's time to leave, we saw everything: one day one of those gringos showed up who hardly ever show their face around the place and spend their time in that office next to the Commissary, shit! he was fit to be tied, bawling out the foremen. He handed them some papers, went into the office and slammed the door, and the next day the Union leaders didn't show up and people were saying that they were in jail in La Ceiba; it's what one of our workers who was from there said. They said they had run them in the night before, they were giving them a goddam work over, starving them and telling them to quit all the shit about communism and if they didn't cut the shit their ass'd be in trouble—well, I'm not sure about the last part. But what I want to tell you is that two trucks full of soldiers from the army came here the same day, they surrounded the packing house and they surrounded us too. It was around seven in the morning and they pointed their rifles at us and told us to get into the carts. We didn't do it, so then the guy who was giving the orders yelled at us again to get in and like again we didn't pay any attention, they started hitting some of the guys with their rifle butts, so then we got scared and climbed in. There, two of them got into each cart with us; we came to the pineapple fields and they made us work. We spent a week like that, and any time they saw somebody slowing down they took him out of the plantation and made him do push-ups or run around the cart. I don't know how it was settled afterwards, but one day the soldiers didn't come along anymore and they gave us a shitty little raise. That's why I'm telling you it's dangerous, because if you don't want to work like they want you to, they'll make you lump it and like it."

"Okay, we're leaving," Luyi said.

The cart was ready to take off, the ten in our crew and the Captain all climbed in. Maybe you'd like to have seen those carts. They were two-wheeled carts pulled by tractors. There were hundreds and hundreds of them in the morning, when it was time to head out for the plantation. They had to leave lickety-split because you can't imagine the clouds of dust the ones in the lead kicked up. You had to tie a cloth over your nose and your mouth, but not your eyes. We liked to see if we were catching up with the one ahead to pass and make fun of them. And the potholes in the road made more than one worker go flying out of the cart and hit the side of the road all banged up. When we got to the plantation the first thing we did was shake out our clothes. We were so white with dust, and every morning one of the guys would say *We look like gringos* and laugh like hell.

Then the Captain would give instructions about the kind of pineapple required that day. Don't think the Captain was a big deal; no, that's why most of them were okay, because they only made them captains so as not to pension them off. And they earned the same money we did, only they didn't go into the plantation, they went around in the cart, watching us work from there.

That day all everybody talked about was the expected strike. The older workers looked worried but the others, including me, were happy, because a vacation with pay wasn't bad at all.

It was almost lunchtime when one of the guys yelled:

"Waaaater, waaater."

I laughed, thinking he was just trying to be funny. Chon saw me looking at the sky and said:

"It means we have to work fast because a foreman or a supervisor is coming, so step it up when you hear somebody yell 'water.'"

A cream-colored car pulled up in front of us: it was the supervisor, who called the Captain, smiled, said something to him and left.

"We have to speed it up," the Captain shouted.

From what I could make out, there was more than one ship in port and we'd have to work late. The ships made us all happy; we knew that when they came in we'd earn more money, and there couldn't be more money than in those ships anywhere. Whenever a ship's whistle, which could be heard all over the city, went into action to announce its coming, everything changed: bunches of kids rushed to the waterside, shopkeepers were delighted and didn't close up till midnight, hookers dolled up to wait for the sailors to come ashore, souvenir vendors shouted and scurried from one end of the pier to the other, and the city looked like another city. In the packing houses, in the offices, in the loading and unloading sections of the pier—everywhere, people talked about the arrival of the ships. It was the same on the plantation; before the supervisor showed up, the workers knew that the ships had dropped anchor. The first one to hear about it whispered to the next guy *Have you heard, the ships are in,* and he'd say to the next *The ships are in,* and this one would say *Luyi, the ships are in* and Luyi went close to Chon's ear and once more *The ships are in* and Chon would slip up as close to me as he could and say between his teeth *Get a move on, work faster, the ships are in.* And by then it was common talk that the ships were in and everybody was singing or whistling. Sometimes the ships were a long time coming and we were all unhappy about it; we'd go down to the waterside in groups and spend hours watching, someone'd climb up a tree and call out *There's nothing in sight,* and somebody else would answer *Maybe tomorrow.* And nobody joked or horsed around, nobody could laugh at anybody else, because when the ships didn't come it affected every single one of us. The city might be a lot of fun but when there were no ships, everything quieted down, even the music. But when people were unhappiest, suddenly, in the middle of the night or at daybreak, they'd hear the powerful whistles waking all of La Ceiba. It was the ships coming back to rid us of our unhappiness.

From then on each one would start trying to see who could cut pineapples in record time, to see if they'd let him work extra hours.

"It's lunchtime," Chon yelled over to me.

"Thanks," I answered and took down my knapsack from the cart where the pineapples we had collected lay stored.

We walked away from the field, went through a thicket down to a small stream where we set down our things and had lunch. The food was a mess because our lunch pails are made of aluminum and with so much sun the food turns sweaty—the tortillas stiff and cold, the rice soggy; and the beans stick to the pail. It was no use taking a fork with you; you had to handle the food with your dirty hands. The stream was completely dried-up and if you washed with the water you carried in your water-bottle, you could die of thirst afterwards. You can't quench your thirst with pineapples either, because Chon says that if you eat a pineapple when you're overheated, you catch a venereal disease; and if you don't have a pass for the infirmary, how are you going to get cured? Chon said he had a pass but he was still afraid to eat pineapples because when the guys checked in sick the doctor didn't believe it was from eating a pineapple. He'd tell them it was because they'd been to the whorehouses, he gave them a rough time and screamed at them that they were filthy pigs.

After eating, some of the guys stretched out, others went in for playing cards and some of us started listening to Luyi:

"Hey, look here, when I was a kid in the village a long time ago . . . well, one day a man got drunk and he was going back home. But he was so loaded that he fell asleep under a huge fig tree, and in the middle of the night a boa constrictor that lived under the tree swallowed him alive.

His curiosity aroused, don Fabian asked:

"And did the guy die?"

Don Luyi looked very serious:

"Well, when the guy had slept it off, he woke up inside the boa and said: 'Where am I?' Since nobody answered him, he grabbed a small bottle of spirits stuck inside his belt and drained it."

All of us laughed at don Luyi's far-out stories, because he told everything so seriously and got angry, if you interrupted him. Don Lelo, on the other hand, was superstitious. He'd open his big eyes and tell stories about dead people who appeared on dark lonely roads, about the weird screams he'd hear in the middle of the night in the hamlet where he lived as a boy, about the gruesome *duende* and the scary Cadejo Negro (a good-sized black dog that grows menacingly bigger right before your eyes). He also said that he knew how to use a Ouija board and that through it you could talk with the spirits of dead persons who had been good; and that he owned the great Red Book, which not everybody could read, because when you were halfway through you heard voices; they threw dirt at you, glass windows shattered, things flew through the air, lights went off and on. He said you had to be very brave to read the Red Book and that he was working to save up money, because he was thinking of going to Haiti where they'd work a cure on him so he could have lots of women and cash.

4

On Sunday morning I took a bath, changed my clothes, and went for a stroll on San Isidro Avenue. I went to see the promo ads at the movie theaters, and apparently *Rambo* was good because the big crowd made the place look like Noah's ark. *Meat fritters, get your hot meat fritters; Oooranges, c'mon, c'mon, they're going but there's plenty; Get in line, you faggot! So's your mother! Then I must be a moron.* Two blacks wearing glasses and carrying a boom box going full blast: *Love, more love, love.* I wouldn't go in; I was in no mood to put up with a lot of racket and decided to go to a restaurant down at the beach.

La Ceiba, where I live, is a retreat for sad cases and tourists. People from Tegucigalpa, San Pedro Sula, Santa Barbara, Olanchito, Siguatepeque, and all the other cities and towns of Honduras are always dying for a chance to visit La Ceiba. When people from other places are going through a very bad time, they have only two alternatives: to commit suicide or take a trip to La Ceiba, packing their cares into the trunk of oblivion. After saying so for generations and drilling it in on the radio and with posters plastered all over the city, the people of La Ceiba have convinced themselves that they are the most hospitable and happiest beings on the planet. Whenever the natives of this city have to leave it—for business, health, studies—they suffer tremendous mental anguish and long to come home to their port. Many students give up the capital and other centers of study only because they can't bear to live away from La Cieba.

La Ceibans single themselves out as the best dancers in the country and are proud to have as Patron Saint San Isidro—custodian of waters and suns—and to celebrate the best *fiesta* in the country: the Grand National Carnival, when neighborhoods and suburbs compete to see which can dress up its streets the best. Barrio Mejía, Colonia Miramar, Sierra Pina, El Centro, La Julia, La Gloria, Barrio Alvarado, San Lázaro, El Naranjal, Buenos Aires, Danto, El Toronjal, La Merced, La Isla, El Sauce, Barrio Inglés, Solares Nuevos, Potreritos and every other neighborhood and suburb—all start announcing far ahead of time that *they* will have the best street decorations at fair time.

La Ceiba grows outward from Francisco Morazán Park, the city's center that's within walking distance of any other part of the city. If you go down San Isidro Avenue, the main street, which passes in front of the park, you can come to the beach at one end, after passing the Dorado movie theater, the San Isidro Market, the Rex Night Club, and many stores. At the other end of the avenue, where it begins, there's the railroad, and a few meters away the Manuel Bonilla Institute and the Young People's Cafeteria. The Cross of Forgiveness is on a high wall almost halfway down the avenue. The Cross has a very special meaning for La Ceibans. The story goes that American missionaries built it and that, annoyed because the people took little notice of it, they blessed it and vowed that on the day the Cross should topple over—the minute it did—La Ceiba would sink; the ground would soften and the whole city would plunge to the bottom of the ocean like a shipwreck. During the rainy season people live in constant fear and plead with Patron San Isidro to use his influence and give them back the sun. Maybe that's why the rain turns La Ceiba into one of the saddest cities anyone can imagine. People follow the tradition of blessing themselves whenever they pass The Cross of Forgiveness. If someone walks past it ten times, he has to cross himself ten times. Years ago, in wintertime, the sea got so rough that it overflowed and reached a long way into the city. Huge groups of Catholics, from adolescents to old people, went down to the waterside to kneel and plead—holding lighted candles and up to their waists in salt water—for the sea to return to its normal state. After two days and two nights of intense prayer, the storm abated and an enormous crowd of parishioners came to offer thanks to the Cross of Forgiveness. Another time, lightening struck the Cross and tipped it over dangerously. Faced with this apocalyptic sign, terror and nervous anxiety gripped the city. For several days the Cross leaned close to the ground; the people of La Ceiba protested to Town Hall and cheered up again only when the Cross was set straight, painted, and redecorated.

14 de Julio Avenue runs parallel to San Isidro Avenue and where it starts you can make out the Cangrejal River and its bridge—not recommended for those who suffer from dizziness at the sight of cracked or missing planks. The river is another source of pride for La Ceibans. They say that any tourist who bathes in it will one day return to La Ceiba. Situated on the other side of the river is what some people call the *barrio* —its real name is Sierra Pina—because the river separates it from the rest of the city. And the students on the 14 de Julio Avenue side, meaning this side of the river, say, talking about the Sierra Pina students: *Here come the villagers.* And in retaliation the Sierra Pinans claim the Cangrejal River as their own.

The street behind the park leads to one of the most popular neighborhoods: Barrio Inglés. From the park you walk
two blocks, starting from the Gran Hotel Paris, to the street
by the railroad tracks that runs parallel to San Isidro Avenue;
then you take that all the way to the pier. Before reaching
Barrio Inglés, you come to a fence that divides Mazapán from
the rest of the city. Mazapán is where the high-level employ-
ees of the Standard Fruit Company—mostly foreigners—live.
Not so long ago, that zone was absolutely off-limits; it was
like a small private city within the greater city. The protests
and the evil looks of the La Ceibans succeeded in making
them put in huge open gates through which the people of
La Ceiba can enter and visit Mazapán. But the fence wasn't
taken down. They also opened the streets of Mazapán for cars
to cross through, avoiding the unnecessary detour down 15
de Septiembre Boulevard—even though that boulevard does
have as its distinctive feature the oldest and most beautiful
palm columns, making it look like a high-roofed tunnel. Also
still surviving in this area is one of the city's oldest radio stations: The Voice of Atlantis. And at the very end of the street
there's a welcome rest stop that everyone knows about: the
General Cemetery. Walking on a few meters beyond the end
of the fence, you come to Barrio Inglés. The surest sign that
you're in it is the vendors' stands in the street, a few steps
from the railroad, almost right on the tracks. The specialty at
these stands is the *baleadas*: black beans and cheese inside a
flour tortilla folded like a half moon. Walking along, you see
places that look suspiciously like the dens of shy bachelors
or husbands who've split up with their wives. Women sit on
the sidewalk in suggestive poses. Their only stricture: that the
customer not be a student. It's the first thing they ask, and it's
not that students aren't allowed to get their rocks off, it's just
that they're stuck with the bad reputation of trying to get
three, and sometimes even six of them, to get fixed up for

one price and with the same woman. It's rumored that some of the students only pay half-price, claiming it's all they have; once in a room, the woman has to accept because her work starts the minute she removes her clothes and the women say that it's better to take off half than strip and then get dressed again for free. Another thing they say about the students is that they stay too long and raise hell if the woman objects.

Barrio Inglés stretches out to where the streets end, near the old penitentiary. They say it was the best prison in the country, because the prisoners could listen to powerful juke boxes from the Barrio all night long and those prisoners lucky enough to have cells facing the street sometimes had the privilege of looking down from their bird-cage windows to see a naked whore chasing after a customer or some bastard of a pimp. Farther along is the pier which fills up with fishermen and tourists. In better times, as many as five ships would come in, but since the actual set-up couldn't handle all of them, the ships had to wait their turn to load and unload. When they arrived in groups, they gave the city a different appearance, making it look as if one of the neighborhoods were afloat. Not so long ago it was fun going to the pier so as not to miss the hustle and bustle of the crates going up and down, or the illusion—in the eyes of all the Hondurans looking on—that the city was striking it rich. The lower part of the pier, between the old iron and the newer wooden structures, has become a place well known and frequented by couples that don't have cash or an apartment. At certain hours, the couples hang around, standing in a line they can't very well hide.

From the park you can also go to La Isla, a neighborhood with beaches and dance-halls. It's called La Isla because it's an island, with only two approaches from the rest of the city: over the bridges or by water. La Isla is in a triangle of water, with the sea on one side, the Cangrejal River and El Estero inlet on the others. The people of La Isla neighborhood love El Estero, perhaps because of its enormous ceiba tree which has given the city its name. Or because people can go to the shores of El Estero alone to think, or, in couples, when they're up to something. At dusk there's a crowd of lovers and people fishing for tiny sardines. The Islanders boast that of the neighborhood carnivals, theirs is the best. The neighborhood carnivals are a kind of teaser, a try-out to give a taste of what the Grand National Carnival will be like the next day.

And on any day the long avenue that reaches across La Isla from El Estero to La Barra is always lively: riders performing tricks on their bicycles; girls in shorts and low-cut blouses; blacks wearing flashy colors, full of rhythm, carrying cassette players—as loud as commercial loudspeakers—greeting anyone who looks at them, *Well Hello bro; byebye man,* never letting the greeting interfere with walking the walk, a walk that's like a dance.

La Barra is the place for discos, restaurants, and stands selling fried fish and all kinds of shellfish soups. Add the sea breeze and the music coming from all directions, and you have all the necessary ingredients for many pleasant evenings by the seashore. La Ceibans down one *Salva Vida* after another till they get drunk; most of them won't accept any other kind of beer because this one is made in La Ceiba. That makes it the best in the world. Each weekend is playtime in the sands of La Barra; bathers of all colors and ages take over the beach. Except on Sundays, when there are soccer games. La Ceibans are divided between the local teams Vida and Victoria, but when either of these two is matched against one from another part of the country, everyone without exception gives the La Ceiban team his complete support.

La Ceiba is flat, spread out; it is a fun city, and belongs to everybody; it is also a hot city, a night city. But people in other parts of the country don't share this impression and when they hear the slogan *Beautiful La Ceiba, the sweetheart of Honduras,* they ask 'And if La Ceiba is so beautiful, why did it pick such an ugly sweetheart?' When La Ceibans hear that, they smile and answer one another: *pay him no mind, this guy is nuts hey.*

Finding myself in La Barra at lunchtime—my morning stroll having enlarged itself—I ordered a beer and fried fish. The breeze was stroking my face; one of Leonardo Favio's songs was on: *Ding, dong, ding, dong, love is out on the town;* I was repeating the words of the song and there in front of me, two tables away, a face was smiling at me, and my heart was like a land-mine at the exact moment the enemy steps on it: *What shall I say to her? If I could only find some pretext; suppose I ask her about, no, no, not that; what the hell would she care that there's talk of a strike. And what if I ask her the time? No, that's tacky; I don't know what I must look like right now, but this is my chance to make my move and I better not miss it because she is really beautiful, and beautiful down below too. I can already see her in a black negligee in the motel down by the Cangrejal River and me slipping it off of her very slowly. But what do I do to break the ice? It's hot isn't it? No, that's old stuff. May I sit with you, gorgeous? Not that either. Have you been here long? Worse, what if she answers 'it's none of your business.' And if I come clean and tell her Miss, I'd like to meet you, be your friend, may I share your table?*

"Yes, of course, that's fine. Sit down."

"It looks like today's my day."

"Because?"

"Well, you've accepted my company."

"I could say the same thing."

"Sure, only philosophers spend their time alone."

"It's also possible that they keep the best company."

"Could be. Your name?"

"Idalia."

"Mine's Guillermo. At your service. Do you mind if we stop talking so formally?"

"Not at all. I'd like that."

"Are you having a soft drink? Wouldn't you like to have a beer with me?"

"One?"

"Yes, just one."

"Okay."

"Where do you live?"

"Close by."

"Thanks for the address. I'll come visit you."

". . . I'm sorry, it's just that it struck me as funny."

". . . that's no problem, I like to laugh too."

"And you, d'you live around here?"

"No, a bit farther away. Look, please bring her a beer and the fried fish and the beer I ordered before, bring them here. Yes, Idalia?"

"What do you do, Guillermo?"

"At the moment I just work."

"That's plenty."

"Maybe not so much, I'd like to go on with my studies."

"But you can go on with them."

"Yes, but not now. It won't be till I'm financially better off, because I want to study in the capital."

"And what are you thinking of studying?"

"Literature."

"It's hard to feed yourself on literature."

"Still, it's what I want."

"I'm sorry, it's not exactly what I was trying to say. And why are you thinking of studying, to teach or to write?"

"Well, what I want to do is write."

"You don't have to wait till you go to Tegucigalpa to start. You could be doing it right now.

"So I have. Just the other day I finished a story I thought was really good; I showed it to a friend of mine, a professor who teaches Spanish, and he tore it apart. He said I started to tell my story in the first person, suddenly switched to an interior monologue, all of a sudden went into straight dialogue in an unacceptable way, and then used the third person, all without a thought to the problems I was causing for the reader. Do you see what I'm up against?"

"Yes, I understand. I've read ever since I was small. My father is a good reader. You can try again."

"Yes, but I'm discouraged. The professor couldn't find one sentence he liked."

"I don't know the professor, but I also don't think he has the last word on it."

"You're right. By the way, d'you know the best thing that's happened to me since I've been working on the plantation?"

"What?"

"The day I went to the office and you almost smiled at me."

"It was no big deal."

"For me it was."

"I'm also very happy to see you again today."

"Do you like to dance?"

"Guillermo, that's something you don't ask a girl from La Ceiba."

"Then I'm asking you to go dancing next weekend."

"I accept. Here's my telephone number. Call me first, so we can get together on it. I have to go now."

"Let's leave together. Ma'am, the bill please."

5

We were working. So far I had kept my secret: What a surprise I am going to give you, old man Chon. We'll see if it's true that those women aren't for the likes of us. I was hoping to go to the Commissary with the old man, have Idalia come along as if by chance, and let him see me talking to her. As a matter of fact, Chon had noticed something, because he had been asking me why I was in such a cheerful mood:

"Aaah, you little bastard, you must've run into something nice yesterday!"

"No, no, Chon, it's nothing."

Just then a fellow worker interrupted us. Since Chon was chewing tobacco and around there the men were always looking for material for their sudden jokes, the guy yelled over:

"Heeey, old man Chon, quit chewing tobaaacco; anybody chews tobacco eats shiiit too."

And with all the workers laughing, Chon answered:

"It's better to chew tobacco than be a big queer like you."

When the laughter had died down, he turned to me again and said:

"I know, you're happy on account of the strike. Isn't that right, dammit?"

"Strike? What strike?"

"What the fuck! Don't you know? Last night there was a Union meeting and they agreed that the Company's time would be up at noon today. If it don't accept, the strike starts this afternoon . . . Ah! Do you want to know who I bumped into at the meeting last night?"

He said it with a sly smile. I was quite intrigued and let out my curiosity:

"Who?"

He just looked at me.

"What?"

"Now you're going to try and tell me that you didn't hear my question."

I explored a thousand possibilities in the next second. Did Chon know her? Had the Olympia team played and had he happened to see me with her? Did she have a husband that he knew?

"No. I know what you're thinking, so I better just tell you. I met her at the Union meeting last night. Well, I already knew her, but we'd never talked till yesterday. She said we should stand our ground about this strike thing, and after the session she called me to ask me if I was your friend. She told me that yesterday you two talked a long time. You bastard, that's why you're so happy, isn't it?"

I smiled but at the same time I got worried: How could she have spoken up like that at the meeting? Isn't she afraid to lose her job?

I didn't go on asking myself; instead I asked Chon.

"Easily, very easily. She works for Standard Fruit. That's true, but she works there because the Union put her there.

Standard has to give the Union some openings for its people. It's part of the contract, see?"

The Union car arrived after our lunch hour. The leaders announced through a loudspeaker that from now on we were on strike. We came out of the fields; they read us a report ... *The walk-out may last indefinitely ... Our objective is an increase in salary, as promised in the collective bargaining agreement signed ... United we shall overcome ... Workers' Union of ...*

Starting then, my fellow workers formed little groups, to talk mostly about the strike; I saw a happy look on every face except old Chon's. He seemed worried and from what he had told me he had good reason to be. What if the Company leaves? And suppose we lose the strike? Who's going to pay us? And what if the Company forces us to go back to work?

Our group also got together:

"We've got to find a little shade. It's about time they let us rest," Luyi said from behind a wide grin.

"Well, yes," don Lelo added, "strikes come from benevolent spirits. In the Red Book ..."

"There you go again with the Red Book," Chon broke in, "Every little thing's in the Red Book."

"Well, the Red Book," don Lelo started in with a threat in his voice.

Fabian came up with his first question:

"And does that Red Book really exist?"

Don Lelo lifted his eyebrows and, opening his eyes wide, he shook his head:

"You have no doubts about the supreme book of all wisdom that's beyond human knowledge!"

Fabian's only answer was to say no with his head. Luyi joked about what had happened to me with the waitress in El Porvenir, and they all asked, almost at the same time:

"Did you lay her?"

"What else could I do?"

Chon, who had now shelved the problem of the strike, said:

"But didn't your pecker fall off?"

Everybody got a kick out of old Chon's retort. Fabian said, as if he were sure of it:

"No, it didn't fall off, yet."

Striking a serious pose, Chon stood in front of me and spoke with a knowing air:

"Guillermo my boy, please explain how señor Fabian Fúnez knows so much about your pecker?"

We were in stitches again, all except Fabian who only wore a sheepish grin.

We kept up our jokes 'till it was time to leave.

"Gentlemen," the Captain said very seriously, "since we're on strike, we now wish to inform you that it's time to go, but we'll have to walk the forty kilometers between here and the packing house."

We were all in hysterics; the Captain's laugh was so loud it made us laugh even more.

We clambered into the carts.

And then I was on a bus back to La Ceiba. The newscaster was giving a report on the strike: *strange ideas have caused the work stoppage; these men who have these weird theories must be punished.* It occurred to me that this is what they say each time there is a strike anywhere.

I got off before reaching my neighborhood; someone had warned me that the army was stopping the buses and grabbing recruits; it was because of what was happening in Nicaragua. All hell had broken loose and Somoza was about to be ousted.

6

I didn't think of this in time. I hadn't counted on the
strike's starting on Monday. And me without cash. Maybe I'd
better not show up. And suppose I stand her up? No, what
would she think of me; no, I'm going no matter what. Idalia is
a very serious girl and wouldn't like being stood up, not a bit.
Aah I've got it; no, not that either. This money business is a
pain in the ass. I'll never change; how could I think of asking
her out without being sure. (This shirt looks better.) Maybe
somebody can lend me a few bills? Ridiculous, absolutely
ridiculous; we're all in the same boat. (What trousers shall I
wear? This pair looks better.) Suppose I made something up,
like I'm sick; that's out, no. I want to see her and she, who
knows, maybe she wants to see me too. Yes, that's right, I'd better not go. Let somebody else call her. Why the fuck can't I
make my mind up? Look, honey, I can't take you dancing
because I have a bum leg. How did I get hurt? Simple; I play
soccer; I'm a forward. We were losing one to nothing, and I
yelled, We've got to tie the game and then win it; we go on
playing; Zorro passes the ball to Pato and Pato centers the ball

beautifully and I stop it with my chest; I lower it; I dribble past one, two, three guys; the crowd cheers; this throws me off but I get past another player; I'm doing one-hundred-and-ninety miles per hour; incredible; the goal keeper hits me with everything he's got and I take off like Superman; I fly over the stadium and the crowd screams at the referee and the goalie; son-of-a-hundred-thousand-bitches; it's a setuuuup; we're gonna kick your teeth down your fuckin' throats; and the referee rules it a penalty; while I crash into one of the stadium light towers; people in the crowd carry me on their shoulders and they roar 'goooal'; and I know I'm the hero of the afternoon. No, this is crazy. I won't tell you this and you wouldn't believe me anyway, Idalia. I don't know how to lie or haven't learned yet. If I only knew you a little better I'd know how you'd like me to act in this situation. How should my face look: tragic, calm, tragicomic, comic? And suppose I ask you to lend me something? That's a laugh! Wouldn't that be wonderful? (I finish shaving; it's a miracle I haven't nicked myself.) It's shit to be broke, but that's not going to stop me from seeing you, baby. This could be the day you're going to tempt me to open my heart to you. (Son of a bitch! I just gave myself the first cut.) It's almost eight o'clock. What a beautiful night. Everything's against me, even the weather; why doesn't it just start pouring; that'd be excuse enough. I'm going to be a little late, anyway; where there's a will there's a way (and I'll take the key with me, just in case).

What could have happened to him? He looks to me like he'd always be on time. I think I'm asking for too much. It's barely eight o'clock; he can't be long now. I hope he doesn't stay away only because he's broke. This would be too bad for a potential writer; he's got to come; maybe he's on a bus, since at this hour the buses take forever. I don't even know why I'm so impatient, really. I haven't felt this way in so long; it's a sign that Guillermo's gotten under my skin. Still, everything depends on whether he comes today. I'm dying to know what he dances like; men are kind of cute dancing. (I'd better go change these earrings.) Whether or not Guillermo comes, I'm going dancing; I'm not staying here all dressed up and in the mood, even if it won't be the same without him; but I always have fun. As long as this strike is on I've got to make the most of my time and not having a boyfriend is a sheer waste. What am I thinking? I hope this one doesn't turn out like Rolando. I don't think so; there's no comparison even as far as looks go; poor Rolando was a big nothing, not even a real person. If I put on some music time will go by faster. I even feel kind of nervous; I'd never have guessed that this lover boy would put me in such a state as this. (This dress isn't right, while he's still on his way I'll try on another.) The thing is, these low necklines are attractive but very provocative and Guillermo strips-you-naked-with-his-eyes. The way he kept staring at me last Sunday, and I wasn't wearing clothes that let him see anything. What a guy! I think somebody rang the doorbell. Am I sure or was it just my imagination? Yes, it was the door. (This bra feels a bit tight, but I'll leave it on. This guy really likes to press the buzzer.)

"It would be nice to walk a little first," Guillermo suggested. "Walking is good for you."

"Aren't we walking now?"

People were going up and down the street. The Saturday evening mood was unmistakable; in dark corners couples merged into one shape. He felt like suggesting to Idalia that they do the same.

"Where do you like to walk most?" he asked her.

"You're the guide."

Guillermo dug his hands into his pockets. In the right he

carried the twenty cents he had on him: "With twenty cents I can't even buy half a soda pop," he thought.

"What's wrong? You look worried."

"No, it's nothing. I was thinking that one of these days I'm going to write something like this."

"Like what?"

"Us. You and me trekking around La Ceiba, and me telling you what I'm trying to tell you now."

She laughed:

"You're off your rocker."

They came to a small park at the edge of the beach. Other couples were rolling around in the sand: "Him on top and her below, him below and her on top," Guillermo said to himself.

Guillermo's brain was in a whirl. There sitting next to him was the girl who had embraced him with her eyes and he couldn't bring himself to talk to her about anything. He chose instead to let his mind wander, to watch other couples, taking a glance at the pier and the sea now and then. He was thinking that if he'd had a few bills in his pocket to spend he'd be capable of anything, of opening his heart to her. Not there in the park but after the dance, because to him the dance was the first step on the road to nakedness. She said little. Not that she was shy or didn't care to talk, but she thought the initiative should be his. She had an idea that the absence of money explained this dead silence, but she wanted to have some fun hearing the excuse he'd give to break up their little trip to the dance. Couples kept passing by and Guillermo's ear caught the hateful words *let's go dancing* from the lips of the girls, and from the guys, very gallantly, *that's just what I was thinking*. But if Idalia asked him, that wasn't what he was going to answer.

The night was perfect, with no sign of rain. He became lost in thought, looking at the moon's reflection on the sea: "They're making love," he thought.

Thirty minutes went by; Guillermo turned the problem over and over in his mind until it seemed silly:

"Okay, I think it's time we went to the dance."

Idalia wasn't ready for this: "Then his being so quiet wasn't what I thought it was," she said to herself.

"Yes, it's time; the sooner we go in, the more we'll dance," she said with a smile.

He screwed up his face into something like a grin:

"There's only one problem," he said, meeting her eyes as he put the twenty cents in her hand, I'm short nine lempiras and eighty cents for the admission tickets."

Idalia let out a heartier burst of laughter than she had in ages, as she told him afterwards. He also laughed and took a deep breath, as if he were dropping a big weight off his back. He felt better now. After a lot of thought, he had managed to say it with such nice words: "The way a writer would," he thought. Idalia gave him a sign and he nodded:

"Then let's go."

They walked along without knowing how they'd begun holding hands. Her laughter reached the empty benches; the other couples had already gone in.

The bass rumbled throughout the dance hall. Guillermo felt as if the notes were shaking him and, taking Idalia's hand, he worked his way through the crowd on the floor and joined right in. The merengue was fast and furious, just the way he liked it. Idalia looked as if any time now she'd drop an arm here, a leg there. The drum battery went on and on and Guillermo was happy because if he weren't almost a writer now, he'd have been a drummer. The dance floor was crammed, a total madhouse; a group of blacks was dancing in circles, each taking his or her turn in the center and those on the edges were clapping and shouting. The vocalist asked: *Are you tired?* and everyone answered *Nooooo*. And the band went into the same merengue all over again.

Guillermo was bathed in sweat. Idalia's face was covered with little water bubbles he pretended not to notice—he had no handkerchief—and her eyes were telling him she wanted to dry herself, and he said something like handkerchiefs had gone out of style. She just laughed. She was having more fun with Guillermo than she had ever had before, because a one-in-a-hundred man like him—she said to herself every five minutes—is what I've been wanting to find for a long time. The heat was growing by the minute, the whole of La Ceiba seemed to be squeezed into the place. But nothing in the world could make the dancers let up. Guillermo said to the dancer next to him: *Please stop pushing me.* And the dancer, smiling: *Sorry, you sound like you're not from La Ceiba.* And a girl's voice: *This fucker just stepped on my corn;* then a big laugh from all who heard. And the fucker: *Go on, go on, it's all over and done with now.* And then the merengue ends.

"You were marvelous, Guillermo."

"Nothing special, but you were really terrific."

"Let's go get something cool to drink."

"Well, okay . . . but for me drinks . . ."

Idalia smiled:

"No, that's no problem. Order anything you like; we'll settle later."

That's how Guillermo liked his beer, ice-cold like in the ads. The singer's voice reached into every corner: *d'you want salllsa, mereeengue, boleeero? Aha, I can see you all want to hold each other tight. Well here goes . . .*

"Shall we dance?" Guillermo suggested.

"It's what we came for."

The brightness in the dance hall went out, leaving low, soft-toned lights. The couples were holding tight, as the singer had said; the song was slow and consequently the dancers' movements were barely perceptible; the close whispering was an unintelligible collective hum. Guillermo heard the couple next to him though: The guy was singing along with the vocalist, softly: *I'm cryyying over youuu.* And the girl: *I just love Jose Luis Perales.* And the vocalist: *I write poems for youu and sing them to youuu.* Guillermo saw that the guy singing softly had stopped at this part of the song, and it seemed right to Guillermo that of all these dancers entwined around each other, none besides himself could write poems. Idalia noticed that other couples danced-kissing-each-other and she was waiting for her partner to press her to him. Maybe not like those she was watching just then in a corner of the room, a couple that look like they're making-love-dancing, she thought, and tried to correct her mania for stringing-words-together when she was thinking. Guillermo was trying to keep body-to-body contact from being too tight. He knew himself well and didn't want to have to put on a look of apology. But Idalia was being provocative. The scent coming from her neck was driving him wild and when she'd lift her face to his, those eyes would embrace him once again. Guillermo was breathing like a scared man. He looked around him. But luckily nobody was watching him. *I'm going to start squeezing you gradually*—he said to himself—*very slowly, so that you won't even notice it.* Idalia had never been much of a guesser but she had a hunch—as they say in Westerns—that Guillermo's arms were closing in on her waist, and *So-you-finally made up your mind, whew.*

After a long, drawn-out *for youuu* that didn't ever want to end, the vocalist brought the song to a close:

"Shall we go out to get some air?" Guillermo asked.

"Sure, it's early; we can walk awhile."

He liked that: 11:00 p.m. and she was saying it was early. And, besides, walking at this time of night? Where to? It had to be to the beach, just the place to get some air—he reasoned to himself—and once at the beach, well . . .

"What are you thinking about?"

"Oh, it's a fault of mine, always going around thinking."

"I have a fault, but it's when I think; when I think, I don't think what I'm saying, I imagine the words and I join them together into a single word. Till I remember I'm slipping into that error and I start separating them. For instance, if I think it's very warm now, I do it like this: its-very-warm-now."

Idalia hadn't known he could laugh so hard. And she hadn't imagined he'd have the chance to do it now, as she watched him bringing his hands to his stomach and laughing as if he had freaked out. It was reason enough to make her tell him where to get off, for laughing at secrets someone told you; but no, Idalia was happy to touch off this big outburst.

"That's enough; you'll wet your pants."

Calming down but still a little out of breath, Guillermo said:

"What an idea, Idalia. How can anybody think or imagine if words are joined together?"

They went down San Isidro Avenue, which ends at the beach. There were mostly young people in the streets, going from one dance to the next; some drunks were yelling, and there was music everywhere. You couldn't tell where it was coming from. A tourist arriving in La Ceiba for the first time on a Saturday night would believe it was coming from the sewers, the palm trees, the sidewalks, or sprouting from their shoes each time they touched the ground in La Ceiba.

"Shall we sit down here?"

"No, it's better closer to the beach."

He wanted to refuse, using the darkness of the place as pretext. He didn't; she might say he was right and later he wouldn't be able to convince her that it really wasn't very dark.

The spot they chose was quite pleasant; the sea breeze was getting into Idalia's dress and she sighed, murmuring something that he understood as *How delicious*. His imagination soared when he heard this; if the air's name were Guillermo it would be stirring up a lot of trouble for her; it would slip into every corner, entering the low neckline of her dress and coming out below her waist. And it wouldn't be bad to sink down between her legs, and then to her ankles— he thought. Some women find this exciting.

"Idalia," he said and moved nearer to her, doing his best to keep his words and his closeness from looking like anything in soap operas, "I've got something to tell you."

She affected a look of surprise:

"What is it, Guillermo?"

"I don't know," he said, acting kind of angry, "I don't know, I don't think it's something to talk about but something to do as the logical next step."

"And do I get the right of approval?"

"Or disapproval," he answered and wrapped his arms around her to enact the kiss under discussion.

After the first one—Guillermo told himself—others and more will come naturally. Idalia was excited, she had thought he'd never make up his mind; as I was telling myself—she reminded herself—the-son-of-a-gun-sure-knows-how-to-kiss; there I go again, dammit. Guillermo was whistling any old tune. He really liked her for more than just a good time. He thought it was really a pity romantic novels had gone out of fashion and were now considered tacky, because he could have written something very good, a masterpiece, about this night he was living through. It had all the right elements: the sea in front of him sounding its waves, the rustling of the palms, Idalia in his arms. "I won't even be able to put in this scene," he thought.

"We can spend another half hour here, then back to the dance, and you can take me home before two, because that's when I said I'd be back."

The kiss and a last feel, along with *We'll see each other on such and such a day* at the door were very important to Guillermo. He believed that anyone who didn't reach those two milestones had no right to expect more. He was walking on air; from where he had walked to he saw the light go out: *sweet dreams and think about me for a little while before you fall asleep, my love.*

7

The weekend had been something special. Maybe that's why I felt like a new man on Monday. The strike was still on. When I came to the place where we take the carts, the men in my group were already there; we all looked at one another pleased as hell, and why not? Nobody was going to do anything but wait for quitting time. Talking, shooting craps or playing cards, happy not to go to the farm to get drenched or fry in the sun.

"Have you listened to the radio?" Luyi was saying just as I arrived, "Shit, those Sandinistas are sonsabitches; they're driving the Somoza Guards crazy."

Greetings interrupted the conversation. Chon, who was bringing some tobacco up to his mouth, looked at me, patted the shaved head of a boy next to him and said to me:

"I want you to meet this country's most brilliant head."

With everyone around him laughing, the boy put out his hand:

"Glad to meetcha; my name's Chago."

"Same here; mine's Guillermo."

Chon held up one hand to show he wanted our attention:

"What you're saying is right, Luyi. They never used to plant pineapples here, only cane. There was a sugar mill where my father worked and where he got to know Sandino."

The older men in the group roared:

"That's enough to make a cat laugh."

Chon looked at Chago for support:

"Well, you went to high school; show us if it's true you learn things there. Is what I'm saying true or not? Did Sandino work and live here in El Porvenir? Yes or no?" Chago thought for a minute, he looked at me out of the corner of his eye, asking me for help. I said yes with my eyes.

"True, I remember now; it's true Sandino worked and lived in El Porvenir. What's not true is that they teach it in school."

The older men broke out laughing again:

"D'you see? We told you," someone muttered.

"I didn't say it's a lie," Chago explained, "What I said is that they don't teach that in school. But I know it because I read it in a history book."

The old guys nodded and threw Chon a look of apology.

"Well yes," Chon went on, "My father used to tell a lot of things about Sandino. He lived in El Porvenir and ate in a restaurant there. He did this on weekends or when there was no work, because work days were the same as now; you had to bring your own food with you. Well, my father used to tell that one day Sandino went to lunch and when he came into the restaurant he saw two gringos eating there and they say he wouldn't eat, said he'd eat later, to let those dogs eat first. And he got out of there; he didn't eat, and other people said he didn't like gringos; that's why he was away from his country."

"The fucker had real balls; that's what men are like."

Lelo nodded, backing up Luyi:

"Shit . . . he had guts; if he was here he'd have licked the pants off of those gringos in the office by now; with a man like that even I'd feel brave. We'd've given him a little hand."

We laughed. Lelo nodded in agreement with Luyi.

"He left here one day," Chon continued, "and after a long spell there was news that General Sandino had died in Nicaragua."

Lelo assumed the look he always did when he was about to talk about supernatural things. He spoke in a voice as hollow as a ghost's:

"He's not dead; I'm sure he's not dead. Those guerillas fighting in Nicaragua call themselves Sandinistas and it's on account of him, because he came back in spirit from the beyond and took over their bodies. He's not dead and he won't die till the whole world forgets his name, and that's impossible; no matter how little known a man is, when his body dies someone brings him back when he remembers or mentions him, especially a man like Sandino, whose name knows no frontiers."

The laughter was not long in coming:

"Lelo and all that crap . . . ," Fabian said.

Lelo opened his eyes in a fiendish way:

"Aaaah, blasphemer, evil tongue, so you question the Red Book that is beyond human knowledge?"

Fabian made a gesture of apology:

"Oh, I really didn't know it was in the Red Book."

The conversation picked up again. Luyi told them that a man in his village had loaned another one fifteen lempiras and went to ask him for them one day when he needed money because he had a son who was sick, and the man who owed him the money said: *Sure, just a minute, I'll bring your fifteen lempiras right out.* And he went inside his house, while the other waited outside the door. But instead of the money, the man brought out a machete and started hacking at the other one, all the while saying, *Look you son of a bitch, here's your fifteen lempiras.* He counted fifteen cuts and then the man he owed the fifteen lempiras dropped dead right there.

"Things worse than that have happened here too," Chon said. "Listen to this: on the road that runs from here to El Porvenir, some guys who were on their way to work found a man's arm on the railroad tracks. They'd gone only a few yards when they also found a child's four fingers. They were scared; they picked up the arm and the fingers and went back to El Porvenir. When I heard about it, I tagged along with them and the police who were coming to look for the rest of the bodies. When we got to the tracks we found the bodies, in a nearby pasture. The man's two arms were missing; he had a gash all the way across his face, and a lot of stab wounds; he was barefoot; his shirt was all red. The woman had a blow on the head; she was naked; one of her tits was split in half; her mouth was full of blood and her eyes were half open. A little farther on was this little girl about five years old. She only had two wounds; one was in her hand; she didn't have any clothes on either; and her legs were spread wide. You know what the ugliest part was? Her little pussy was covered with blood . . . When I saw it, my nerves got the best of me. I thought I was dreaming. Other people who also went to look lost their voices. Some women cried. The medical examiner who came said they'd killed them to rob them."

"What evil sonsabitches those killers were," Chon protested.

"How can there be people like that in this world," Luyi agreed. Don Lelo was thoughtful for a minute and said:

"They're not people of this world. Those who carry evil in them are not of this earth; they're messengers of darkness from Lucifer."

These last words made Fabian's blood run cold. You

could tell from the hair on his arms standing on end for a good while.

"And why are you going around with a shaved head?" I asked Chago.

He smiled:

"They fucked me up, man; I was drafted."

"Where do you live?"

Over by El Pino."

"Okay, but what's the name of the place?"

"Well," he said, looking down, very embarrassed, "it's a new settlement and doesn't have a name yet."

"Aah," I answered, seeing the spot he was in. To help him over his embarrassment, I added:

"Tell me something about your time in the army?"

"Well . . . there's a lot to tell and . . ." he looked at the group one by one to see how curious we were.

"Go ahead," Chon encouraged him, "We've got all day to sit here talking, so tell us about your hitch in the army."

Chago told stories about corporals and sergeants, screaming lieutenants and days of everlasting sun, orders hard to carry out and punishments nobody'd ever imagine, hungry recruits breaking down, shaved heads and purposefully visible wounds, firing positions and obstacle courses, impossible exercises he never failed, Sundays restricted to the base and Mondays that offered hope, deserters and students killed in so-called accidents. Hearing it all, Lelo envisioned enormous cauldrons on kitchen ranges, red flames and thousands of souls pleading for mercy and trying to get out of the boiling water. He could see *duendes* with yellow eyes and pointed teeth roaring with laughter and using a skillet to push down souls trying to escape from the huge cauldrons. Chon thought about protecting his sons, about the past when there had been no draft, and about talk he'd heard that fists and kicks and being kept awake nights and insults shouted out in public was part of the training. Guillermo imagined green phantoms trying to trap him, orders for his arrest and threats to shoot if he didn't obey, long streets, bruised feet, running for his life, green phantoms hot on his trail, *Halt, Report for duty,* sweat, *Stop I tell you,* turning the corner, more green phantoms, doubling back and jumping over a fence, guns trained on him, *Are you or aren't you going to stop you son of a bitch,* clenching his fists and taking a fast look at his pursuers, *Idalia, I'll never see you again,* putting on more speed, *Goodbye ma they're going to kill me, Halt you animal,* a dark alley, puffing hard, silence, I fucked them and lost them and they'll never catch me. Luyi was listening with rapt attention. He put himself in Chago's shoes *and that day they threw us into the river at 4:00 a.m. and the water was like ice and the fucking cold seeped into our uniforms and me wishing I could fly to get the hell out of there and they threw us off the same bridge again and if you were scared they clubbed you till you fell in, and always the fucking cold.* Fabian listened and looked at Lelo as if he were trying to guess his thoughts, and he couldn't in the least suspect what Lelo was thinking about all the things they were hearing but he felt he agreed with whatever was going through Lelo's mind anyway. Chago finished his account, making a big deal about how well he had passed firing practice, how all the others kept missing, how tough they were on them, *And just me looking on and laughing because I never wasted a single bullet.*

I'm facing Beti. It's nice facing her and knowing we're colleagues. We're two first-rate conspirators. We've been mixed up in this for a long time. And we like it and we need it. At one time, you could go far out of the city alone, to the country, to the river. You didn't have to hide from anybody to think. This is a drag, it's the end, the limit, they could have banned everything else, except thinking. Who doesn't like to think? We all like it, or maybe we don't like it, maybe it's just that sometimes we have to think; it's necessary, to save us from dying. And I don't know why it is that when they ban things, these become more interesting. If they ban a book, let's say, even if you're not in the habit of reading, the minute you find out that reading this book is an offense, you go in desperate search of whatever it is they're so set on keeping from you. Beti looks at me as if she's scared. She knows, she's very sure of the terrible violation of the Law we're committing right now. She knows what can happen to us if someone has seen and denounces us. Still, both she and I were desperate to have some time to think, to be alone with ourselves.

8

On my way home I got off the bus early, since they were still pulling in recruits. I took a cab; they're not very safe, but somewhat more so than buses. Without young men around, the city seemed empty and silent. The cab driver turned on the radio you hear in all taxis. I felt a little nervous. After what Chago had told us, anyone who let himself be drafted was an ass. The patrols were on the sidewalks everywhere. I thought perhaps they'd go away later and then I'd be able drop in on Idalia. It was still early but it was beginning to grow dark . . . *half past six; greetings to our friend the driver tuning in to us in cab number forty-seven and to answer the request of* . . . I felt like getting out near Idalia's home. That's what I was debating when an army truck parked on a corner and guys started to get in. My mother was waiting for me. She was worried, and when I told her I was going out in a little while she got worse and went on and on: *You boys should fix it up with your girlfriends so that during drafting time they visit you. Just think that if they grab you, how am I going to get you out? Remember that when you're poor nobody listens to you.* I finished supper; it wasn't eight o'clock yet. To kill time I started to read: *Anita was a model girl in everything, until she took to hunting insects. She was the best student in her school, was well mannered, knew how to do so many good and nice things, and her friends were the best in our society . . .*

At a few minutes past eight I rang the buzzer at Idalia's and her mother came out, *What is it, young man?* A handsome, smiling lady. *It's for you, Idalia.* Idalia came to the door. *Come in, Guillermo, how have you been?* And I went in. What a nice house, a big well-furnished living room, Hi-Fi player, TV set, decorative objects everywhere, it was nothing like my place. I sat down on a piece of furniture. I felt like someone from outer space. The mother disappeared through a door and we were alone in the living room. *Where's your father?* Idalia brought me a soft drink. *He's gone out; he won't be long.* I'd never been in a house like this. Everything looks fragile and you're afraid that you will accidently break glasses, decorative objects, ashtrays . . . And as for the things that won't break, like the furniture and the curtains, you don't want to touch them either because they look like they'll soil at the slightest movement. During one of many times Idalia got up I checked my shoes and, lucky for me, they weren't too dirty. She went over to the stereo, *Would you like to hear some music? What kind of music shall I play for you?* I was thinking that to look good people ask for classical music, and not knowing what else to say I pronounced that little magic word and the noise of the violins and the saxes broke out in my head (in those days the sax was the instrument I liked best, maybe because of its similarity to the word sex). Idalia asked if Schubert was okay and not knowing the goddam difference between Schubert and Herbert, I said it was all the same to me. Idalia told me she'd been waiting for my call and had been thinking that I wouldn't show up. When she said she had been thinking I imagined *he's-probably-not-coming* and I laughed, and as she was burning with curiosity, I asked her if when she had been thinking she hadn't run the words together and she laughed *So that's it, making fun of me, huh?* and our laughter raised the roof. First we talked about the dance last Saturday and agreed that we'd never had so much fun and would attend others very soon. We mentioned the strike; she said they expected a solution within the next few days and there was no reason to be upset, that the Union was strong, that the Government's policies encouraged these companies to feel that they owned the country . . . I didn't go on listening because my blood turned to water when I remembered I was there strictly to declare my feelings, to see if she'd accept me as her boyfriend, because we had kissed on the weekend, but she might have done it just for kicks. I believe she noticed that I was pale. *Are you feeling sick? Are you all right?* I was very embarrassed that she had noticed something; no, it's nothing, and she, relieved, *You looked kind of strange.* And my smile returned, *You're probably just seeing things,* and we laughed softly. Her father arrived, Idalia rushed to open the garage door and when he got out she covered him with kisses and they came inside with their arms around each other. *Look, dad, I want you to meet my boyfriend.* I felt my knees turning to water, my feet told me to take off on a marathon run, my heart was leaping so hard it seemed to bump against my chin, *Pleased to meet you. What's wrong? Do you feel sick?* I sat down, words wouldn't come. *Give him some water,* her father said. After the water I was able to smile again and, *Thank you, but don't be alarmed, it was nothing.* The door through which the mother had disappeared moments before now swallowed her father. I wanted to leave so as to be alone and think about the big hit I had really made with her. Idalia showed no sign of being sleepy; we talked about an infinite number of subjects. I told her about Chon, Luyi, Lelo, Chago, and we laughed at the funny things I told her each of them said. We kissed goodbye shortly after her father went from one bedroom to another in his pajamas, yawning. *Don't pay attention to him; that's the way dad is.*

Because the two of us are apparently here, together. But no, Beti has gone off; and so have I, each to a different place: What's left of us here is our bodies. And nobody can stop this; the Law says: Anyone who thinks, dies. I believe I'm alive, at least that's what I take for granted now. Perhaps not. At worst, Beti and I may be dead, dumped on a roadside, covered with blood, bruised, beaten to a pulp, in the process of decay. Dead. Faces disfigured so that no one may identify us. This could be a dream, seeing Beti and seeing myself in this place far from all suspicion, far from the imagination of those who are allowed to think; it will never enter their heads that this is the third time this year. On each occasion Beti and I leave the city to take cover in this cave for hours on end and think in absolute silence. It will never cross their minds that someone has dared to defy authority, their authority. Beti and I are heroes: We plot, we provoke, we call ourselves the opposition, rebels. We ignore the radio and newspapers and television: Avoid problems, obey the Law, don't think if it's not allowed. If you wish to think without breaking the Law, apply for your voucher today. Beti and I don't need that damned voucher. Voucher, false permit, the waiting for death.

9

The strike looked like a fair. Laughter, whistles, shouts, and people milling about. Many portable radios were going full-blast, reporting on the war in Nicaragua. Workers formed large groups around anyone who had a radio and listened quietly, as attentively as if the news were a soap opera. In other groups they talked about the war. The workers gave their different versions and most of their faces reflected deep concern. Somoza's fall was the topic of the day and the removal of the other president who had replaced Somoza for a few hours had become the butt of endless jokes. Guillermo was giving his version of what he had heard on the midnight news: *They said that the Guards had cleared out in droves, terrified, running—throwing down their guns and pulling off their uniforms—this way, to Honduras. And they say that the Sandinistas have already taken over the country and there are thousands dead in the streets and the town squares. And they say that the people are happy, burying their dead and celebrating the triumph of the revolution. And I heard it live when they passed because a Honduran station was able to intercept guerrilla communications; they were saying Eduardito, Eduardito, answer Eduardito, it's urgent. Can you hear me? Eduardito, three four two, Eduardito. I hear you, speak louder, please, I hear you. Eduardito, Eduardito, go over to the other side, come on down, come down all of you, everything is alright here, just about all over. Can you hear me, Eduardito? Yes I hear you. Did you understand me, Eduardito? Sure, everything's okay, over. Over and out, Eduardito. And in the background you could hear explosions and people screaming. And they also say that a lot of Somoza Guards switched over to the guerrilla side, that many others were taken prisoner and that the airport in Tegucigalpa had barely been able to keep up with so many airplanes landing with refugees going into exile. And they reported that when one of the generals got to the airport he ripped off all the medals and stars on his uniform and said,* This shit is no good anymore *and dumped them in the trash. And many countries had sent notes of congratulation and offered all available help to the revolution. And they were saying that health brigades from many countries were coming with large quantities of medicine to take care of the thousands of wounded. And they said the whole country had been destroyed and not a minute must be lost in rebuilding it. And in Tegucigalpa people were gathering in enormous groups in the main streets where they had set up huge loudspeakers and television sets to hear and watch the news. And the whole country was happy over the triumph of the Sandinistas. In Honduras they were celebrating Nicaragua's festivities almost as much as in Nicaragua. And after the following commercials we'll return with more information.*

Everyone laughed at Guillermo's clever way of getting even the commercials in. Others told of similar accounts they too had heard on the radio. Everyone wanted to contribute and the workers' excitement reached such a pitch that they seemed to be describing an action-packed movie everyone had seen and enjoyed.

Lelo sighed and everyone was quiet, knowing this was a very peculiar way he had of announcing himself before talking:

"Thanks to the Divine Master that the war in our sister country has come to an end."

Taking some tobacco out of a piece of newspaper wrapping, Chon said:

"I hope that's true; war is never any good."

Chago, who was some distance away from the circle, joined it and sat down:

"Who knows? I think the war is just starting there now."

"Why?" Fabian asked, frowning as if he didn't understand a thing.

Chago hesitated:

"Well, I don't really know. But a man from over in El Pino, who went to the university and knows quite a bit, was saying that the war is just starting now."

Luyi, who was fanning himself with his hat asked:

"And what did this university guy say?"

"Well," Chago said, eyeing them all with suspicion, "I'm not too sure of this"—he leaned over toward the center of the group and dropped his voice—"He says that now the war will be against the gringos, because they're not going to want a government that's not on their side."

"Aha," Chon said, "I know something about that, but not a whole lot. Only that my father knew Sandino and the gringos didn't like him because he wouldn't let anybody shove him around."

Lelo raised his eyebrows and, holding up his hand like an imitation Christ, said:

"Man is still a long way from obtaining peace; he doesn't have the wisdom necessary for him to forget war."

Guillermo adopted the look of someone who knows more than the others and explained:

"I didn't want to say anything, but since I have to, I will. The university man Chago's been talking about is right: the war is starting now. Don't you see that it was the Americans who kept Somoza in power?"

Luyi put on his hat:

"It's very clear."

"I figured it was something like that," Chon said.

Before speaking, Lelo threw Fabian a meaningful glance to keep him from asking any silly questions:

"The Red Book talks about all this, about the power the bigger countries have over smaller ones; but it's not going to last. Some day the small countries are going to rebel and with the help of the Divine Master they'll destroy the beast and the beast will feel pain in its naked flesh and will want to die but will not be able to die; this will be its punishment, to live in the eternal flames of hell."

Fabian nodded again and again, as if to leave no doubt that he was of the same mind.

"I'd like to see that Red Book," Guillermo said.

Lelo looked shocked:

"It's not easy to read that book, and not just anyone is allowed to read it. Forget what you said, or else the curse may fall upon you this very night."

Guillermo felt like laughing but he kept a straight face:

"If that's how it is, I won't even think of it, Lelo."

Lelo sighed, as if he had just escaped death by a miracle.

Chon was smiling innocently. Luyi sat with his head between his knees, meditating. Chago had lapsed into silence. Fabian opened his eyes wide, as if he were seeing something horrible. Guillermo was thinking of the war. Lelo looked at the sun, figuring out how much time they had left before this day of the strike would end.

10

"Why don't we go for a walk around town?" Chago suggested.

"It wouldn't be a bad idea," Guillermo observed, "I like El Porvenir."

"As long as we stay close to work," Chon warned, "there's no problem; I've had enough of this town, but I'll go with you."

"Walking is good," Lelo encouraged; "knowledge of the good is acquired by walking."

"But we mustn't stay away too long," Fabian suggested; "the bosses keep their eyes peeled around here."

They agreed to follow the railroad tracks. Chago carried nothing; the others had their work equipment with them.

They walked in pairs, each talking about different things.

"Are you going to look for work here on the plantation?"

"No, I'm leaving in a week."

"Where to?"

"To the capital, to Tegucigalpa. I'm going to go to the university; an uncle I have there is sending for me; he found out they drafted me and prefers me to be there."

"When d'you think the strike'll be over?"

"I can't imagine when, Luyi. But I think they're going to settle it soon, because there's lots of ripe pineapples."

"You're right; the longer the strike lasts, the more they'll lose."

"And does he come out in the daytime?"

"No, only at midnight. He gets here riding on a horse."

"So if you want to write why don't you go there too? This isn't the right place for a writer."

"I don't know, maybe I'll make up my mind some day to go; but first I want to write something to take with me, to make things easier."

"Right, it doesn't pay for the company to hold out, because when the pineapple is too ripe by the time it gets on the ship they won't accept it. The strike has to end soon."

"The Union says they won't give in till they get the raise."

"And have you ever seen him?"

"Whew, once; no, I've seen him several times. The horse is black and he's dressed in black and sends fire through his eyes."

"I'm going to tell you a secret: I'm going to write a novel about the plantation."

"Don't worry, I won't breathe a word and thanks for trusting me."

"Noooo, I've been in worse strikes than this one."

"But they all end okay, right?"

"And suppose you run?"

"That's the worst thing you can do. When you bump into an evil spirit you don't run, because if you run you're letting him know that God's not with you, and they take advantage."

"But don't they kill people?"

"When I get there, I'll try to get you some writers' addresses so you can send them what you're working on."

"Yeah, we'll write to each other."

"Some strikes are dangerous. Shit, it's so damn hot my whole back is soaking wet!"

"This is some crazy climate; it hasn't rained since the strike started."

"It's fucking bad for the crop."

"And what can you do when an evil spirit jumps you?"

"It's simple, throw Psalms three-seven at him: 'Arise, O Lord; save me, O my God; for thou hast smitten all mine enemies upon the cheek bone: thou hast broken the teeth of the ungodly.' And you make the sign of the Cross; you'll hear a howl and the spirit will vanish."

"Loook, loook," Luyi and Chon, who were walking ahead, called out together.

The others ran up. On one side of the tracks a snake was pulling itself along.

"It is a boa constrictor," Chon muttered knowingly.

Lelo, who had even lost his breath, contradicted:

"No, it's Lucifer in the form of a beast. He will bite your heel and you shall destroy his head. What are you waiting for?"

"For what?" Luyi asked.

"To destroy it," Lelo answered. "We mustn't let that evil creature live, because it can bite some unsuspecting Christian."

After Lelo's words, rocks of every size rained down on the snake until they gave up the animal for dead. They went on walking and fell into the same order as before. Luyi stopped to take a leak. Chago joined him, saying:

"Spanish pricks need company to piss."

And all the others suddenly felt like taking a leak.

The tracks ran on in a straight line from where they were till you came to El Porvenir. Trees framed its sides and a variety of birds sang all along the way. The leakers finished and moved on. Guillermo and Chago, who brought up the rear, decided to bet on who could hold his balance better walking on top of the rails.

Chon and Luyi chatted on, suddenly laughing now and then. Lelo was saying something to Fabian, who listened with his mouth hanging open and his eyes ready to leap out of his head.

The streets were deserted. Occasionally a woman went by with a pail of water on her head or a bundle of wood under her arm. Several men of advanced age were in the house yards, some just sitting there, others doing light work: planting flowers, watering the portion of street in front of their house; or lying in a hammock, smoking tobacco. You heard a horse neighing, a dog barking, a rooster crowing and then the silence would return.

"This place looks like it's dead."

"It's not dead; divine peace is like this."

"You can't call this divine peace."

No one said anything else and the town was once again as quiet as if they had just killed it, with merely the sound of their shoes tapping on stone. The sun was melting them. The sweat on their foreheads resembled the spermlike wax of candles about to sputter out. A very old man, swaying unsteadily on his feet, was coming toward the visitors. When he saw the nearly transparent figure approaching, Lelo felt his hair stand on end and, gripped by a terror that he couldn't hide, he quickly mumbled the Lord's Prayer backward and forward. Chon grinned:

"There's no reason to be scared; it's Pachán, a man who never bothers anybody."

In spite of these words in the man's behalf, Lelo crossed himself. Guillermo and Chago exchanged looks and clenched their jaws to keep from laughing. Luyi was smiling and talking to himself, with his head down. Pachán's slow, lurching motion as he advanced made him look like a blind man groping for his cane. As they walked along, they could hear the surf getting louder and were starting to feel the breeze.

"Hey, hey, friends," Pachán shouted with the voice of a movie drunk.

Everybody stopped. Chon, the only one who knew him, answered for them all.

"What's up, Pachán?"

"I've got one bitch of a hangover; buy me a little drink, man; have a heart."

The men in the group looked at one another and nobody showed any sign of having money. Chon put his hand on Pachán's shoulder:

"Some other day, Pachán; we're all cleaned out today."

"Not even enough for one little drink?" Pachán insisted with the voice of a movie drunk, "Just enough to get rid of this hangover I woke up with."

Luyi begged off:

"No, Pachán, some other day; and besides, you don't have a hangover, you're drunk now."

"Just a little drink," he insisted again. "Shit, and I thought you were my brothers."

Chon was all for walking on. Pachán leaned on a fence and started to cry.

"If I had any money I'd give it to him," Fabian remarked.

The others said nothing, to let it be understood that they felt the same way.

When they got to the beach, Chago came up with the idea that a dip wouldn't be bad; Luyi and Guillermo agreed. The entire length and breadth of the beach seemed theirs; not a human shadow was anywhere in sight, so they were able to swim with nothing on. Lelo kept Fabian from joining the bathers, warning him that it was very easy for Lucifer to go into the sea because it was so enormous and deep. Chon only smiled at each of Lelo's superstitious notions.

The bathers were hurdling the waves and yelling as they thrashed in the water, much to the envy of Lelo who didn't really believe Lucifer would go into the sea. He didn't know how to swim and was ashamed the others would find out. Chon decided to hunt for crabs. Avoiding the temptation to join the swimmers, Lelo invited Fabian to walk along the beach. A little later they all got together again for lunch. Chago had nothing to eat with him and stretched out under a tree. The pineapple pickers were in the habit of each sitting alone and apart so that no one could see what any of the others had to eat.

"Do you all know that there's one of us who didn't bring along any food?" Chon asked.

Luyi backed him up:

"There's food for everybody here; where there are men no man starves to death."

Nothing more was said. Chon, whose lunch pail came in sections, one on top of the other like floors, emptied one of these storeys and everyone came over to put something in it. In no time, Chago's lunch was ready. He thanked them, half-embarrassed, and joined them.

Chon's voice made itself heard again:

"Now that we've finished eating I want to say something. We can't quarrel among ourselves from now on; we're like brothers because we've seen one another's food."

They shook hands to seal the deal. Someone suggested going back to the strike because Lucifer never sleeps. They walked abreast down the middle of the narrow street. Fabian was saying how much El Porvenir looked like his home town. Guillermo pretended to listen. He was thinking of the problem he'd have later on, when he tried to describe El Porvenir. He had read novels where they described small towns, but none like this one. In those books there had been towns where the mayor, the local policeman, the druggist and the shopkeeper were characters, but in El Porvenir those characters were nowhere to be seen and nobody talked about them. Looking deeper into the problem, he discovered that the heroes in this town were, in order: Marel, the driver and the owner of the bus with the La Ceiba–El Porvenir run; El Chaparro (Shorty), the center forward of El Porvenir's soccer team, who played with number ten on his shirt; don Raul, who had a son studying in Tegucigalpa; Luisa, who had been to bed with all the men in El Porvenir and any others that passed through; Mauricio, the local singer who had made it big in La Ceiba's night clubs; and the dozen students who traveled to La Ceiba's schools every day. Guillermo wasn't sure that his prospective readers would believe in this El Porvenir. Yet he felt sure that describing the place had a lot to do with describing the people, since there wasn't much to say about the town itself: one main street almost always empty, the biggest general store, which wasn't even a real store, the town hall with its very old mayor who was a compulsive pool player, the jail with its chief of police and his three assistants that spent most of their time in other towns because everybody in El Porvenir knew them too well for them to be able to pull in any extra money here.

They reached the tracks; each one looked for his partner and paired off as before; they headed for Montecristo.

"I told you the secret about my novel and I'm going to tell you another, but don't you let it out."

"Sure, Guillermo, I'll be as silent as the grave."

"But don't evil spirits drown in the sea?"

"How can you believe that? Only Divine Power can make evil spirits vanish. Listen carefully: vanish—not kill."

"Don't you have watering problems with what you've planted in your garden at home?"

"No, Luyi, because a stream runs close by and it's easy to fetch a few bucketloads."

"That really is a big secret. Congratulations! And since when have you been going with her?"

"Since last weekend; her folks know about it."

"And then a huge black bulk, shaped like a dog, appeared in front of me: it was *El Cadejo*."

"What else could it be? Lucky for you it didn't kill you."

"That gal is gorgeous. You won't get mad, will you? When I looked at her, I ate her up with my eyes. Not now, because she's a buddy's girl, right?"

"Okay, no problem; and do you have a girl?"

"I'd like to read the Red Book."

"Don't go around saying that; have you read the Bible?"

"But I have watering problems, because where I live the river is fucking far."

"Don't let it upset you; maybe the rain will come before long."

"I don't have a girl; but I know two sisters, they're both scrumptious. And I'll be frank with you, they're not for me to get serious with, they're good for getting laid. I'm after one of them and I've almost made her. Why don't we do something? We'll go see them when you get off; you can hide that bag somewhere along the way and I'll introduce you as a cousin who's from the capital."

"As long as it won't be a waste of time, there's no problem as far as I'm concerned."

"Yes, you have to read the Bible first because the Red Book has two sides to it, one good and the other evil. If you start reading it without knowing the Bible, the evil side gets you and you're damned; when you die, your soul belongs in Hell. The Red Book and the Bible can work together, but only for the good."

"Yes, right; shit yeah; the pineapples in that area were really something."

"You're talking about the area near the highway; they seem to grow better there than anywhere else. We're almost back."

"No, man, it'll work out with those two. What I've needed was somebody to take care of the other one, because I'd be lying if I said I could handle them both. They live alone in that house, and to show I'm thinking of your end too, this is what I'm going to do: Since I'm already getting somewhere with mine, I'll ask her to go for a short walk to the river; it's not very far, and you can stay with the other one; you take it from there. Here's a last piece of advice: These girls like you to be kind of rough with them; the rest is up to you."

11

The two girls were very good looking. Following Chago's advice, Guillermo had combed his hair and was now saying a lot of things like *It's so hot in this place,* and the girls didn't know what to do with this guy from the big city. *Would you like some candy? When are you leaving?* And he remembered Chago's advice: *Say you're leaving tomorrow to her so she won't lose any time.* Chago and his girl were already on their way to the river when he came back to Guillermo and handed him something, *In case of emergency.* Guillermo told him, *Thanks;* he was feeling okay now; but he took the little packet. The girl was curious and asked what it was, and the city guy, smiling, *Oh, it's nothing; they're pills for the heat.*

"The capital is so far ahead of us!"

"What's your name?"

"You're awful; you've already forgotten my name."

"No, I didn't forget it; I didn't hear it."

"My name's Juliana; you talk so nice."

"And you, you're so cute."

They spent thirty minutes sweet-talking each other. Guillermo remembered *When you've talked to her for fifteen minutes, you should have kissed her at least once.* He pretended he was tired:

"Let's lie down a little bit."

"D'you think just because you're from the capital I'm going to go to bed with you?"

"No, precious, I'm not interested in you; I meant lie down dressed, without touching each other."

"I don't interest him, he says; then get out of my house!"

"Okay, don't get mad; you're beautiful."

He stroked her hair and followed this with a kiss. She clung to his neck and his hand slid down her waist and when they reached the end of the skirt they moved upward again in direct contact with her skin. Kissing and touching, they walked to the bedroom. They stripped and she asked him:

"Suppose you get me pregnant?"

The city boy smiled; he reached for the small packet Chago had given him and said:

"This is a condom; it's to keep women from getting pregnant."

"The capital is so far ahead of us!"

The night's caught up with us," Chago said. "How'd you make out?"

"No trouble at all. And you?"

"Same here. All she needed was a little nudge."

They shook on it. Guillermo started to worry; a dark night and they were far from the plantation.

"I know a short cut but it runs through the bush."

Guillermo didn't like the idea very much but he gave in when he remembered that he still had to catch a bus. They went into the bush. He shuddered at every sound. Night birds were singing; so were the crickets and other insects.

"There aren't many yellowbeards around here, are there?"

"What do you mean! Sure there's plenty; don't you see we're near the foot of the mountain? But don't be scared; all you've got to do to keep the snakes from biting you is walk fast. Don't think I'm brave, but we've already gone too far to chicken out now; besides, for those two sweet, round asses anything's worth the trouble, don't you think so?"

"Sure I do. The one I had is something to brag about."

Chago was leading; the road was too narrow for them to walk abreast; he jumped back a step and cried out:

"Shit, look, look at that light there ahead."

Guillermo felt all his hair bristling like needles. He was shaking; it was cold out but they were both soaked in sweat:

"It's a cat," he said in such a timid voice that it made Chago feel even more scared.

"No, it's not a cat; if it was a cat it would have two lights; and besides, it's not moving."

He gave Chago the benefit of the doubt. Behind them, a branch broke and they didn't know whether to go ahead or double back. Chago didn't believe in zombies or ghosts but, trying to muster courage, he said:

"It's a dead person!"

"No, dead people don't come back."

"What can it be?"

They were quiet, saying nothing to each other; but they were waiting, stone still, for the light to disappear. After some minutes of high anxiety and the shakes, another light came on next to the first. The two lights moved toward them; a chill seized them both and they huddled close together to keep each other warm. Suddenly, with a miaow, the lights moved away at top speed. They walked on, deciding it was a cat on the prowl and standing sideways so that only one eye could be seen. They had a few lesser scares and finally reached the plantation.

There were no buses or private cars; the place was deserted.

"Oh I know, the freight train will come along any minute now and you can jump on."

Guillermo didn't think that would work out:

"We're on strike, remember? There's no harvest; what would the train come here for?"

Chago got up:

"Let's go down to the railroad."

The tracks were dark:

"Be patient," Chago advised and he bent down; he laid an ear on one of the tracks. "Nothing, I can't hear a thing, but we've got to wait."

While they talked, Chago would now and then get down and listen, and after what seemed like a hundred tries, he got up and said:

"Bend down, listen, the train's coming."

"And what can it be coming for?"

Chago smiled:

"To pick you up. No, it always comes. When there's no pineapples to carry, there's material to take to the storerooms in La Ceiba."

They said goodbye; both smiled when they recalled how well they'd made out with the two girls.

"Hey, heeey, get down there. Don't you see you're going to fall off? . . . Get down, get down, I don't know why you people like to hop on for joyrides," the man in charge of signalling the conductor—better known as the brakeman—shouted.

From the top of the last car, Guillermo shouted back:

"Look, mister, I'm not just going for a joyride . . . I work here on the pineapple plantation; I missed the bus . . . I have no way to get back; please take me."

The brakeman said nothing for a minute, then he answered:

"No, no, get off; that's what they all say... Then they get killed and I'm the one responsible."

Guillermo insisted:

"Please, mister engineer,"—he knew prefectly well that he wasn't the engineer, only the brakeman, but he also knew they liked to be called engineers—"I'd really appreciate it if you could take me, mister engineer."

The brakeman shouted:

"Alright, ride there, but hang on good. How far are you going? If you're going close by, let me know so I can stop. Don't go throwing yourself from the moving train... Don't forget, hang on real good."

After the explosion of laughter:

"Well, from what I can see, you got here fine," the grandfather said.

He smiled. He was pleased that his grandfather gave him so much attention without ever seeming bored. The old man rose from the chair in front of the hammock where his grandson was telling his story.

"I'll prepare something to eat and you can continue talking to me later, because I think you're hungry, after walking all day."

"Yes, grandpa, that sounds fine; whatever you think best."

The grandfather lit the wood in the small stove:

"Everything you've told me is so interesting."

Guillermo laughed:

"And there's more to come. . ."

"I know that," the old man said, putting a pot on the stove, "I can't wait to hear more about Idalia and Chago and the others. But you're tricky, you hold back to make me go on listening to you."

Guillermo was rocking himself in the hammock. He was inspecting his grandfather's cabin very carefully; then he went on to think that it wouldn't be a bad idea for this cabin itself to be part of the scenery of his novel, part of the general atmosphere, he corrected himself. And his grandfather could be another of his characters. He relished the idea, because the cabin was easy to describe: it had only four walls covered with cracks, some very old pieces of cardboard thrown into a corner, the hammock, a bunch of bananas hanging from the middle of the ceiling, the tamped earth floor, and a mouse that poked its head through a hole and hid again when he heard their voices.

"This is ready now."

Guillermo took his portion, his grandfather did the same and sat down:

"We can go on now, boy."

Perhaps Beti and I are among the few who have been able to think so far this year. Civilians must not, under any circumstances, think. But Beti and I are willing to run the worst risk: torture. Talk, you son of a bitch; talk, you slut. Who else thinks besides you two? Who are the leaders? Where do you have the thinking manuals buried? How long have you been thinking? Pass me the hood, you moron; don't just stand there looking stupid. And how should I answer to *Why do you think?* For sheer pleasure. *You're lying, you son of a bitch! Where did you receive training to think?* Nowhere, we've never gone out of the country. *You're lying, you slut! Why do you think?* We think so as not to forget where we're from and who we are, to laugh at the laws, to stay out of reach like birds, to decide what we'll do to fight on equal terms against those who deprive us of the right to think anything we want. *Kill them! Make it look like an accident! Take our newsmen to the scene with cameras and television crews!* And Beti and I appear, our bodies covered with evidence. The evidence is simple: As you can observe in the photograph (extreme right), the bodies are surrounded by manuals on thinking methods, the same they (the criminals) used to threaten the authorities who pleaded with them—almost on their knees—to surrender, to put down their manuals.

12

One week after Chago left, the strike ended. At 9:00 a.m. that day the Union people—including Idalia—showed up and had all the workers meet under a tree. Naturally we couldn't all fit there; as I was telling you before, there were thousands of us. Over the loud speaker, one of the Union representatives said that the strike was over, that we hadn't obtained all of our demands, but that we had gotten fifty per cent of them, which was already a lot, and at the next negotiation we'd get the rest. Right away you could hear the hum of tractors everywhere and everyone in my crew climbed into the cart and we left for the plantation.

"We spent almost three weeks whacking off," one of our guys said.

"Well," another said, "everything is worth something. I had time to clean up my whole corn patch."

"What corn patch?" Monkeysdream laughed at him, "You don't even have a place to drop dead in."

Another backed up Monkeysdream:

"Corn patch? What he's got is a tiny cow pasture without any cows."

Everybody laughed:

"You can tell a jackass by his laugh," the offended man defended himself.

We all laughed again and split up to go into the plantation. "Those guys love to hassle each other; some day they'll kill each other," Fabian said.

Chon, who had a chunk of tobacco in his hand, set him straight:

"Who says they're going to kill each other? I know them and they spend the whole day like that, but just let somebody else go poking fun at them and they'll kick his teeth down his throat."

There were a lot of ripe pineapples. We filled our huge sacks without having to go very deep into the plantation. We loaded the cart in no time. Luyi remembered Chago out loud and we all talked about him.

At leaving time, the Captain called us together:

"You guys are in luck."

Surprised and happy at the same time, the ten men in the crew exchanged looks. The Captain went on:

"The ships have arrived; from tomorrow on, we'll work overtime and this whole crew'll come in at 6:00 p.m. and leave at 2:00 a.m. So get some sleep during the day tomorrow."

I didn't quite understand all of it, but I joined in my companions' happy shouts anyway. Later Chon explained that there was higher pay for night work and, apart from that, the hours seemed shorter because there was no sun.

The first night of work seemed excellent to me; we were in the middle of the plantation and the headlights of the tractors provided us with light; time really flew by. We had a snack at around eleven o'clock; Luyi and Chon carried large thermos bottles of coffee; I learned to smoke because my fellow workers said it was the only way to keep the mosquitos off. My companions worked and sang. Nobody in my crew lived in La Ceiba; that was my one problem; I had to walk to where I took the 4:00 a.m. bus. I had to cover seven kilometers on foot. Can you imagine what a bitch it was, going down that dirt road alone? You feel the chills right down to your balls. When you want to take a short cut across the plantation, you're in real trouble; you walk a little and fall into a mud hole. And if it's raining it's worse. You jump at every thunderclap, at each flash of lightning you shrink back into yourself; before you know it you slip or else get your legs all scratched up in the shrubbery; and since you can't see a thing in the pitch dark, crossing some farm you're liable to crash into a cow. That's how you get to the highway. From there you still have to walk another long stretch and cross the bridge over the Bonito river, near where Luyi used to live. If you tend to scare easily, you'll never make it. Along the side of the highway you'll find a lot of crosses for people they've killed; owls hoot overhead. Although you're not credulous, you remember the guard whose head they sliced off to steal his pistol, the man a tractor ran over, the one slashed with a machete, and other things they say happen around there. And as you pass over the Bonito bridge, you feel desperate. You wonder if it's true La Siguanaba appears to men here, and right then you hear an owl and your heart's down in your shoes. But you can't run. You think that if you do, something may follow you. The whole place is so dark, every sound makes your flesh crawl. There was nothing left to do but put it out of my mind and think of payday, of Idalia, or remember Chago, or think of a joke, or something. I've never really believed in ghosts. But I believe in the deeds of the living, in someone who could rob or murder me by mistake, because these things happen. There have been cases where somebody who has an enemy lies in wait for him at a spot he usually passes; you happen to come along; he's nervous; he gets mixed up and kills you.

The first Saturday we were to get paid for the night shift plus the days of the strike. We were all very happy. Nobody knew exactly how much we were going to get, but we figured it would be a pretty good amount. We arrived in the morning, real early, to wait for the paymaster. We'd been to the Captain's first to pick up the pay chit, and I was furious. Look, the chit said: *Hours of work: 40 (forty)*. That was for the night shift; then for the days of the strike: *Hours of work: 0 (zero), Economic assistance, Total. Received and approved.*

I showed it to Chon:

"Don't let it get you down, kid. For poor people like us, this is just one of many insults we've got to take every day. It would've been worse if they hadn't paid us anything."

"That's right," Luyi confirmed. "We have no one to turn to."

"There's no reason to waste tears," was Lelo's opinion, "The beasts that run the world gradually fall one by one. Good will conquer evil. The Satanic beast will not succeed in blazoning his emblem, the three sixes, across the globe because before then those that are humble will obtain the wisdom to defeat the powerful forces."

"That's true," Fabian said, "that's very true."

"You're young," Chon said, "You still have time to continue studying and not have to spend your whole life like us, living a life of shit."

The others in the group agreed.

"People think working here is nice," Chon went on with a bitter expression on his face, "Tell me one thing: How can it be nice? You're born, live, and die. There's nothing else. All we do is die on the plantation. Look at me: here I am, sick and tired of working so much; I've been working almost since I was born. Where I come from, you work in the fields from the time you're a runt. You don't go to school, because that's not what the old people understand. They say: I didn't go to school and I live alright. Stop and think, Guillermo, whether that's really living alright. My advice to you, since you're young, is you'd be better off studying—but not to be a doctor, or even worse, a military man. Study to be different from all the engineers and doctors who were students like you yesterday and today are the big bosses fighting one another for position, biting one another and fucking the likes of us who're nothing.

"There's my sons—you know them—I send them to school to improve, to be human beings. I don't want any of my sons to be bank managers. If they use their jobs to make a living, that is alright, but without cashing in. Because that pisses me off. You see, the bosses always have the best women. They take advantages of you any way they can and if you don't like something and say so, they kick you off the job and everybody looks down on you; they say you're a communist. Sure, that's who they're scared of most of all. Me, I really don't know much about this communism thing but they say it's ugly because communists share things. Now, to a poor bastard like me it's all the same and sometimes I think it may even be better. D'you know why, Guillermo? Because if it means working and sharing, it's good; and us, don't we work all our lives? And what have we got? Nothing."

Every one of us approved but said nothing. Luyi got to his feet:

"We might as well go stand in line, even though nobody's there yet."

There was no one else, just the five in our little group; some others were playing cards for money and getting into debt for when pay time came.

"C'mon. Later you'll have a hard time getting your pay," Chon yelled over at them.

"Wait, old man, I'm cleaning these guys out," Cowhump answered.

"Cleaning them out," Luyi commented, "And the most they bet is twenty cents."

"All the better," Lelo advised, "Lucifer hangs out in places where there's lots of money."

"That's true," Fabian said.

"I wonder what our wild friend Chago is doing now?" Luyi said.

"They say Tegucigalpa is one helluva place," Chon put in, "Right now he's probably going around with sore ribs from climbing up and down so many hills."

"And with swollen feet," Luyi added, "And a stiff neck from looking up at so many buildings."

"And you, how come you're not talking much?" Chon asked me and turned to the others, "This guy is tied up with one of those girls that are too good for the likes of us."

Lelo moved his lips, speaking softly: "Such a pot must have such a lid. To each his own."

I waited for Fabian to nod his head like an idiot and say "That's true." But he said nothing.

"I was just listening to all of you," I told Chon.

"Don't try to fool me; I noticed you were in the clouds. Well, love makes the world go 'round."

"And does she pay you any mind?" Luyi asked me.

"Woman, like the serpent, strikes without warning," Lelo said.

Fabian nodded and, as I had expected before, said:

"That's true."

13

Maybe today everything will work out for me and Idalia will finally give in. It may be tacky of me, but the truth is, you've got me head over heels in love, worse than Romeo. I want you in body and soul, though I'd be happy enough if it is only in body. I want to know your nakedness, your shudder at the exact instant of ejaculation. Reading isn't a bad thing; thinking in words that aren't mine. If you hinted that you wanted to feel me inside you, that would be fantastic. Today I want to explore deep inside you. I sound like a poet stunned by the muse. You can't leave me before I try you out. I don't know how, but it's got to be. The danger is that afterward I won't be able to pull away from you. I have a feeling that I love you though I don't like to admit it. If you only knew that I've been ready for half an hour, that I'm killing time sitting here in the hammock in the yard. I won't lean back because then I'll have wasted my time ironing these clothes. And writers shouldn't be like me; no, they're probably more emotionally developed and they don't fall in love. Anyhow, I think falling in love is still something good, even if one loses the con-

*dition of intellectual control. I don't know why I'm thinking
all this nonsense. What do I know about intellectuals? They
must be flesh and blood like me, kind of green and clownish
now and then, serious when occasion calls for it; some are
good, others selfish and untalented, and there must be all
kinds, like in every group. Ever since I read that pamphlet,
what's it called, oh yes, that's it, "The Commitment of the Intellectuals," I've been turning it over in my head. I'll have to
read it again to understand it better. Only a few minutes past
seven. The more you want these watches to go faster, the more
they slow down. I'm going to try to organize my mind and
think about something other than that sunovabitching pamphlet. As if I cared that much about intellectuals; I don't believe I do. You must also be ready by now, Idalia; no, I doubt
it; women need forty-eight hours to get ready. I wouldn't want
to be a woman, except maybe for one thing: to have a baby
and spend three months of maternity leave not working.
That's the best part about being a woman, vacations for being
pregnant. I'd like to work the night shift for a long time; my
money goes further and, as the professor says—I guess he must
be my friend after all—I have to read. And with the dozen
books I bought today, I have enough to last me a couple of
months; but I must keep on buying even if I don't read them
all at once. It must be a lie, or is it the truth—that to write all
you need to do is read? All readers would be excellent writers
if that were true. But till I find someone with more experience,
I'll listen to the prof. Idalia will love knowing that I bought
these books. She will love it even more tonight when we get to
know each other without any clothes on. You're going to get it,
my darling; I'm not much of an expert, but after the magazines and porno movies I saw as a kid, I'm not so dumb either.
I can't stand waiting this long. What can I do? Perhaps I'll
start walking slowly and stop along the way to buy her a little
gift. Great idea, and what shall I give her? Women love*

flowers. What a shame that offering flowers isn't hip anymore. Maybe it's not what you give but how you give it. Better yet, I'll give her one of the books I bought plus a flower. Not a bad idea. You're a genius, Guillermo. Okay, don't let it go to your head.

I think I got dressed and put on my makeup too early. Guillermo is-driving-me-crazy, I mean, is driving me crazy. If he doesn't like me in this pink dress, he has no taste. I should talk to him seriously today, ask him what he thinks of me. No, all girls ask questions like that and being a potential writer, he must detest everything trite. I've never felt so excited about anyone I met before him. Maybe he's worth it. He's so serious and kind, but when he looks at me as if he's taking my clothes off I feel something—I don't know what—that starts at my ankles and runs up to my throat. Maybe it's just plain desire. What am I saying! This low neckline will give him the all-clear. If he doesn't catch on so-much-the-worse-for-him; there I go again. Because of him I even forget other things: I didn't call the compañero *at the Union for the latest report; luckily I still have time. I'll call him later. Right now I'm enjoying thinking of you more than anything, Guillermo. I hope it's the same with you. In the meantime, I'm going over to the mirror. This is the right one, yes; there's no two ways about it, this-dress-is-beautiful. I did it again. When will I ever get rid of this habit of joining words together? A few minutes after seven. You'll be ringing my door bell any time now. After all this business with the Union I think I deserve a nice evening out, dancing, for instance, like the other time. Meanwhile, I'm-going-to-read-for-a-while; there I go again.*

They had been to the dance. He asked her to go for a walk. The evening had given them time for everything. At 7:30 p.m.

when he went to pick her up, she was ready and they decided to see a movie and then go dancing. They entered the theater without looking at the promos. Once inside Guillermo felt himself turn red: the film was porno. Idalia seemed to watch without concern. Whenever the scenes got hot—when the blond girl peeled off her clothes and started moaning and caressing herself, with the blond guy spying on her and pulling down the zipper on his pants to masturbate—he didn't know whether or not to watch. Then the blond guy flopped down beside the girl while she looked surprised for a second, until, spotting his erection, she started to stroke his penis.

"Let's go," Guillermo suggested.

"Okay," she answered.

They got up and were walking out when the audience came to life, whistling and yelling, *Hey, they couldn't hold out. Let her finish seeing it so she'll learn. Hey, don't forget to pay for a room because if the cops catch you fucking standing up they'll get your ass.* Guillermo was absolutely pale and perspiring with shame.

They were heading for the beach now. He figured it was almost 11:00 p.m. and he hadn't asked her to go to the room yet. He was sure she wouldn't get away from him and he was thinking that if *I come from the capital* had been magic words he'd have said them a long time ago.

They sat down where they had the last time, on the beach, taking in the breeze. They had wanted desperately to be alone from the minute they started kissing. *This guy's coming on stronger than ever,* she said to herself. Guillermo was biting, he was sliding his hands up and down. *If she doesn't protest it'll be worse for her,* he thought. They were like that for almost forty minutes. He was happy, excited; he hadn't gone as far as he wanted, but at least he'd invaded her low neckline and had run his hand up a little above her knee; those were big steps. She had also done some *sinful* touching, as her mother would have said, straightening her out. He figured that if this wasn't the right moment to take her to bed, there wouldn't be another:

"Let's go to . . . " He was afraid to continue.

"Where?"

"Oh, nowhere; it's hard for me to say it."

"It doesn't matter, I know what you mean. Let's walk to where you want us to go."

They went to the apartment a friend had lent him so he could make out.

"Do you rent this room?"

"No, it's a friend's, but you can make yourself at home."

By the dim light of a lamp, moaning and sighing, they got lost in each other. An hour later:

"That was something special."

"Yes, it was special," he sounded terribly sad.

"Is something wrong?"

"No, it's just that I'm so touched."

He thought of many things, especially of the chance that Idalia might never mean anything serious to him. Perhaps he'd never go to bed with her again. He was annoyed that she hadn't waited for him to draw up the courage to do the asking, but had gone ahead and done the asking herself. He wondered how many others she must have done the same with—and he had stupidly wasted so much time courting her, even giving her flowers. From now on he wouldn't treat her with such tenderness but just like one more of the women who had been to bed with him. He had no desire to talk or make love again, wanted only to get away, to lose himself in his solitude.

Or they'll put on a show live, in full color: machine guns, grenades, bombs fired again and again at the house where we're supposed to be and where we hide the manuals for thinking. And we, stubborn suicides, don't surrender. So they riddle the whole house with gunfire, and after twenty hours of intense bombardment they give us up for dead and find us side by side, purple, cold, giving off a stench, each with a single bullet through the heart. And everyone will wonder, had we committed the greatest crime of all: thinking? Their propaganda instructs that if you think you're an atheist, anyone who thinks usurps the Kingdom of God and the wages of sin is death (after torture). And your relatives bless themselves: Thy will be done in our country as it is in Heaven; Thou hast given us life, Thou takest it away. And Beti and me on the front pages, stained red all over, Beti's black hair streaked red, the manuals intact, without a drop of blood, only some fingerprints that aren't ours. And me with my eyes closed as if I am thinking about impossible things, eyes closed as if I'm saying to myself: you didn't kill me, fuckers, I got away from you to go on thinking forever. And the text under the pictures will say a thousand things; they'll reconstruct the accident. They'll deceive no one; I've done the same thing the man they found on the city outskirts did. It's the only way to die: let everyone know who the guilty ones are; find some way to give a signal, a cry, anything that will reach the eyes and ears of the people.

14

Chon cut a pineapple from its stalk:
"One more strike and Standard Fruit will leave."
"It won't leave," Luyi said.
Guillermo pulled his glove off:
"I've already answered Chago's letter."
"And what did you tell him?"
Guillermo blew on his hand:
"Not much; it was a short letter."
Chon dropped a pineapple into his sack:
"I see you acting strange, Guillermo. You're not like you used to be; at noontime you don't have lunch with us anymore; you go off to read."

Taking advantage of the fact that his sack was full, Guillermo went toward the cart.

"I'm telling you, he's lost his head over that girl."

"But she returns his feelings."

"Yes, but what's not for you is not for you, and there's nothing you can do about it."

"That's true."

"I hope he gets over it soon, because I love this bastard like he was my own son."

"Guillermo remembered that a few days before Lelo and Fabian had traveled to another part of the country where Lelo owned a piece of land on which he was going to plant coffee.

"I wonder what Lelo and Fabian are doing now."

"Maybe right now Lelo is lending him the Red Book," Luyi said, letting out a guffaw.

Chon stopped smiling:

"It's about time the evil spirits grab Fabian by the hair and parade him around the whole town."

The three of them laughed heartily. Chon pulled a handkerchief out of his pocket and mopped his forehead:

"Shit, it's so hot! You wouldn't think we were about to begin December."

"This heat is a bitch," Luyi remarked.

"That's why I wish we could always work nights," Guillermo said.

Chon put his handkerchief away:

"Well, boy, you don't know it but staying up all night is bad; it makes you get old quick."

Luyi stuck his hand under a pineapple:

"And here the heat is nothing compared to what the guys in seed-planting have to put up with."

After throwing a pineapple into his sack, Chon took out a chunk of tobacco:

"In seed-planting it's really fucking tough; they put you to work. You have to plant fifteen beds by yourself, each about fifty meters long, and each with two rows of pineapples. Some workers have almost died there, because the sun sucks them dry."

Guillermo pulled out a cigarette:

"Well then, it's a good thing we're here."

Luyi was walking to the cart:

"That's right, it's a good thing, because we'd be worse off anywhere else."

Talking and chewing at the same time, Chon distorted his words:

"Well, who knows; when you get down to it, it all comes to the same thing."

"Don't you believe it; the seedbeds are murder," Luyi said raising and tilting the gallon jug of water to his mouth.

"Oooold Maaaan Choooon, stop chewing tabaaaaco . . ." Cowhump yelled over, but Chon interrupted him:

"You must have your intestines instead of brains in your head, the way your mouth always comes out with the same shit."

Everybody laughed; they were almost two hundred meters apart, but they always shouted things from one side to the other as if trying not to lose contact. Whistlemouth shouted:

"Hey, little shit, how do pilots stick their hands out to drop bombs from those planes that fly so fast?"

This was a reference to an incident Luyi got into. One day army planes had flown over so fast that they barely got to see them and Luyi, who was still behind the times, happened to ask that same question. To defend himself now, Luyi answered with a long guttural sound, in imitation of a ship:

"Poooooooooo . . . poooooooooo . . ."

"You ought to know about fast-moving hands from all the jacking-off you do!" Chon shouted.

Everyone laughed at the joke, except Whistlemouth who was left trying to think of another point of attack.

They went on working in their different directions.

"We made them shut up," Chon said.

Luyi glanced at Guillermo:

"Only you don't say a thing. You don't help defend the group."

"Next time; they didn't give me time to think just now."

Chon was chewing, Luyi was whistling a Mexican tune and Guillermo was smoking a cigarette. They were walking side by side and, at each step, they would put one hand behind their back and drop the pineapple just cut into their sacks.

What is Guillermo thinking about? Maybe about that woman. If he told me about it my advice would help him. We're not old for nothing. Luyi's head is also in the clouds. He's working next to me as if he wasn't here. Must be the heat because the fucker's a killer; my whole back feels wet; and who knows what time it is; maybe it'll soon be noon because my gut's getting itchy; and I didn't leave my kids much to eat. You've got to have balls for this; the little money we get here isn't even enough to kill my family's hunger.

I'd like to see you, Idalia, to ask you to forgive me. But I can't get up the nerve to do it. If I were only a little braver and had the same courage—to ask your forgiveness now—that I had when I fucked you. I don't know what I'm going to do. Mama is right when she says that you don't know the value of things until you lose them. Maybe if I gave you a call everything would change. That's what I should do. I'm going to think it over carefully. After all I won't lose anything by trying.

Chon is staring at me like a stranger, Now he's looking at Guillermo. What's wrong with him? He must want to chew the fat; seeing us so quiet he feels left out. If he only knew that I don't even feel like breathing. This sun has my whole ass soaking wet. If Lelo were here I'm sure he'd say it's so hot there's going to be an eclipse today. But today, Lelo, I can finally see that it's my fate to die on this plantation, even if I don't want to, because however little you earn here, it's more than what they pay a construction worker, a carpenter, or any other job outside the Company. Others are worse off than me. I hope that my sons don't have to go through this, that they study like Guillermo who, sooner or later, will go off somewhere else to make it big. Somebody like me has a tough time just learning to read. That means no future. Still I believe it's worse for Luyi who doesn't even have kids.

I don't believe Idalia could have found someone else yet. Maybe luck will be on my side and she'll still be waiting for me. But what can I offer her, after I've already acted as if I didn't trust her. And at this pace who knows how far I'm going to get with my novel; the poet told me—almost begged me— that to improve my skill I had to read and write every day. What'll I do? My head's no good anymore for thinking of any- thing but you, Idalia.

He must be way off, in the mountains, and Fabian right behind him listening to all his wild fantasies. Lelo can turn anybody's brain with all his crap about Red Books and Divine Powers. Looks like this heat's going to kill me. I feel as if they're pulling my skin off. Could I be sick? Guillermo doesn't even wipe off the streams rolling down his face. Maybe it's really not too hot after all. Balls! Chon is feeling it just like me; all this sun's fucking him up.

Maybe Luyi read my thoughts. Why did he look at me like that? Maybe he looked at me same as always and it's just me feeling guilty. Whether he reads my thoughts or not, the truth is the same: getting to be an old man like him and without having any kids is a damn crime.

If I could write something like what's in the magazines that the poet loaned me, and if I gave it to him to send out and they printed it, maybe I'd have a little more courage to speak up, Idalia. It's tough, the poet knows I've got some potential but says I'm far from being ready.

Lucky for me I have two; even if they're always pestering me they're still a source of joy. It's nice to come back from work and have them waiting for you. If it wasn't for those two kids I'd have passed on by now or I'd have turned into a drunk.

I wish I didn't live in Bonito anymore. Maybe Chon could make it easier for me to move to El Porvenir, because Bonito's dangerous with so many drunks. So many goddam thugs have moved in there, I don't know, I'll make up my mind one of these days.

Idalia would accept me if I made up my mind to talk to her, I'm sure of it. I'm going to stop all this shit and drop in on her any day now.

Luyi looks like he's talking to himself, and this boy never seems to stop thinking about that woman. They ought to be like me, only thinking about my kids.

Chon's been looking at me for quite a while as if he wants to tell me something. What's the matter with him? When I write my novel I'm going to tell this story about me and Idalia, even if the poet, that damned poet, tells me love stories are too old-fashioned. There has to be some way of bringing it up to date.

"Tiiiiime," they heard the Captain call.

The three snapped out of their reveries and went to look for the lunch bags hanging tied to the top rim of the cart.

15

It was the second time he visited the poet in his consulting room. Guillermo waited his turn in the outer room. There were two others there with him, a man who wasn't very old and a woman with a lot of greying hair. The man was very quiet, as if he were ashamed; one trouser leg was drawn up above his knee, exposing a blood-covered wound. The woman sat bent over herself, motionless and silent as a statue, with one hand covering her forehead and eyes; she was slowly stroking her stomach with the other. Guillermo heard the poet's voice, *Next, come in,* and the man who wasn't very old struggled to his feet and hobbled into the consulting room just as a boy came out, rubbing his hip. Inside the clinic, like everywhere else, the heat was unbearable. Guillermo noticed that the woman's face was streaming and that the drops were dripping onto her dress. *It looks as if she were crying,* he said to himself. The moans of the man being treated reached the waiting room. Through the window you could see the street where the pineapple workers were walking home slowly, their footsteps heavy with fatigue. A young black parked his bicycle outside the clinic and took down a basket he was carrying on the rack in the back. Guillermo came out to see what he was selling, bought himself two banana cakes, and sat down on a railing. When he finished eating, he went over to a tap in front of the clinic and quenched his thirst. In spite of the heat beating down on the place, the water was cool. *Hi, kid,* he heard the poet say.

Sitting face to face with the poet made him uncomfortable because he believed that when speaking to him you had to put on a refined tone of voice, have a faraway look from time to time as if you were alone with your thoughts, not wave your hands around too much when you talked, and use unusual words: *pragmatism, utopia, sceptical, promiscuous, presumption, virulent, thesis, discern, irrelevant, testicle, mujik, slogan, in fragranti, incautious, Constantinople, pubis, n'est pas, ce que, conjugal, visceral...* The poet smiled at Guillermo's vocabulary, so strained because he was nervous, *because he was young.* He would correct this later on. The poet was talking about the tap out front that Guillermo had drunk from a moment ago. He was saying that he was thinking of writing something about it, *because, people apart, an endless number of animals have drunk water here: horses, birds, dogs, snakes, and even insects. This tap is always important. I believe I can come up with something very important.* Guillermo asked him if one could write about mysterious things. *Well, in my opinion, no one can stop you from doing it, but personally I think that it's something no longer valid. It's better to write about reality, about what we see and live through. I mean literature should fulfill a social need, and this you young people, more than anyone else, should keep very much in mind.* The answer seemed correct to him but it also made him sad. He was thinking that there would no longer be room for Lelo in his novel, since the Red Book was something mysterious and contrary to reason. The laughter the poet was holding back almost escaped at the next question: *Do poets fall in love?* After a discreet smile, the poet smoothed his hair with one hand, *They're flesh and blood; I believe that they, more than anyone else, need a muse.* Guillermo liked that little word a lot and was already playing with it: *Idalia is my muse, I have to see my muse.*

Guillermo got to his feet. He paced up and down as if he wanted to say something. The poet pretended not to notice; he started going through some papers he was holding so as to let Guillermo get up the nerve to say whatever was on his mind. The poet was reminded of the leading man in a TV soap opera who paces a hallway smoking, waiting for the doctor to come and tell him, *Everything's fine, it's a boy.*

It wasn't long before Guillermo started spelling out his romance with Idalia, gradually providing a detailed account of everything that had happened. The poet advised him to go see her and let her know what a mistake he had made. And Guillermo recalled the night they had made love for the first and only time, how, as he left her, he had told her she was cheap, he hadn't believed she was like that, he never wanted to see her again, and the expression of fear and surprise on Idalia's face when she answered, *But what have I done, Guillermo? Are you crazy?* and her rush to disappear into her house. In spite of the poet's encouraging advice, Guillermo was afraid to face her. He thought he'd never be brave enough to go to her house, let alone talk to her, that the last look in her eyes—which no longer embraced him—had been the unhappy end of their romance.

Straining his wits to help, the poet mentioned couples who had gone through worse situations and ended up back together, inseparable. As an example, he told him about Marco, a local from El Porvenir who, in a fit of jealousy, slashed his wife with a machete and then went to see her in the hospital; she immediately forgave him, and now they were rejoined as if nothing had ever happened. Guillermo's hopes flicked back and forth rapidly, like a flag hoisted on the beach. Two hours later he said goodbye to the poet, who, from the window, wished him *Good luck, kid.*

16

There were few enough people on the bus taking him to La Ceiba for him to travel comfortably. Through the window—he always liked to sit next to the window—Guillermo could see the enormous pineapple fields they were passing. The bus's slow progress let him watch how people on bicycles caught up with the bus and then left it far behind. From the highway the pineapple plantations looked *very beautiful* —as a tourist one seat ahead of him said—totally green with white stripes that were the little lanes used by the carts.

The plantations began at the edge of the highway and ended at the foot of the mountains, *Pero las hondureñas están en el gloria con tanta riqueza,* Guillermo heard a gringo say in poor Spanish. *That would be if they belonged to us Hondurans,* a pineapple worker in the back said and everyone in the bus laughed, including the gringo. *Ella tiene mucha razón, a mi me parecía que las siembros de Honduras eran de las hondureños.* The answer came from the back again: *The farms that don't grow anything belong to the Hondurans, but those that grow pineapples, bananas, grapefruit,*

114

oranges, all belong to the Standard Fruit Company, and loud laughter filled the air again. Silence returned once more, all they could hear was the radio: *From the love and good living station, greetings to the ever-popular Chema, down at the beach selling fish from very early in the morning, love and good living, and going out to the last caller, the lovely Nancy, here is the winner of the OTI TV song festival of nineteen seventy-eight.* Listening to the disc jockey speaking so fast, he remembered Idalia and her habit of stringing her words together when she was thinking. The song filled the bus. *Played by the marimba of the kids from . . .* A passenger near Guillermo was singing along: *While his mama scrapes along from day to day, Quincho works like a plow horse to make ends meet.* And you could hear the gringo's voice once more: *¿Aquí ponen el música comunista? Long live Quincho, Quincho Barrilete, boyhood hero in my home town.* This time the answer came from the front seats, *This American's really a pendejo. Long live all the kids who come from where I come from. ¿Qué ser una pendejo? A living specimen of poverty and dignity. Long live Quincho, Quincho Barrilete.* A man wearing a suit and tie answered: *A pendejo is a very good man, his name will never be forgotten, because in the streets, squares, parks, and neighborhoods people remember him.* The gringo listened to the song and protested with a *Sunuvabitch.*

We've just finished listening to Quincho Barrilete, by Nicaraguan composer Carlos Mejía Godoy, sung by . . . The American muttered to himself, *These damn Hondurans.* The man in the suit remarked so that the whole bus could hear him: *It's a beautiful song.* And in the front seats a woman said: *I saw it on TV when they gave out the awards.* The American spoke again, *A mí no importar esa canción.* A worker in the back answered: *I don't give a fuck if mister don't like it.* Guillermo thought the American would be better off if he'd shut up. If he went on they'd never stop heckling him. Not that the pineapple workers had mean intentions but, when it came to Americans, they didn't distinguish between the good and the bad ones. Any gringo who talked nonsense became the butt of their jokes. Now more than ever they were opposed to the Americans because there was a rumor going around that one of the American big shots in the office had held a gun to a worker's mouth. *Your favorite station, deep in your heart, sending out love . . . and good living.* Silence had settled on the bus. Guillermo remembered when, a few days before, he had tried to make up with Idalia. He had admitted to her that he had acted stupidly and she had answered that she knew it, what she couldn't understand was how a man who said he was going to be a writer and claimed to have progressive ideas could do what he had done to her. Where was his new society, his equality among men? Guillermo was stumped. He didn't know what to answer. She ranted on without pity, telling him that with minds like his, the country would always be backward. He had really disappointed her. She hadn't for a second thought that he was just another freak. Why hadn't he told her about his active interest in extreme machoism? And just when he had found an explanation and was ready to make it clear that it had all happened in a jealous fit, she hung up on him. Now he was thinking about how the poet had told him that these things were never settled over the phone, that it would be better if he went in person, that trying to clear things up by phone was just a way of feeling guilty and being a coward at the same time. *Esta país ser una infierno,* he heard the American's voice. *Well if you don't like it you can go eat shit, you Yankee faggot,* Guillermo answered without knowing how or when. The people on the bus sided with him, saying yes, the American ought to get out of the country if he didn't like it. One of the passengers came out in defense of the American. *Stop fucking with the very people who help us out most by coming to visit us.* The whole bus protested immediately: *Yes, there's always somebody around who sucks ass; they ought to throw all those shithole lappers in jail; he's talking crap so the gringo'll feel sorry for him and give him a dollar; not even snakes sink as low as that guy.* The man who had defended the American was in the front seats. He stood up and, putting on a brave front, challenged anybody to fight him. And then all hell broke loose: fists flew, screams and sons-a-bitches came from almost everybody's mouth. The driver stopped the bus, the passengers started to hit the brave guy and the American and ended by throwing them off of the bus. *Let's get going and leave the two assholes here.* Then the entire bus heard the voice of the American who, turning to the brave guy, said *Todo pasó por esta indio que se meten donde no la llaman,* and the other one: *Ahh you fuckin' gringo, I'm defending you and you throw that shit at me?* And he was all over him. The bus had been pulling away but stopped again. Several people stepped off to get the American away from the brave man, *Let's take him with us before the guy kills him. But the gringo's to blame; no, both of them are, him for acting like a faggot and the other for sucking ass.* And the bus moved off, leaving the brave guy in the middle of the road making *lewd* gestures at the passengers, as the man in the suit said. The American's mouth was bleeding; two women were attending to him, one of them saying, *This serves you right for opening your big* buchaca, and he was in pain but made an effort to ask *What is a* buchaca? One of the workers let him know, *Your big mouth, stupid.* Guillermo was surprised at himself; he didn't even know how he'd happened to answer the American and spark the uproar. He wanted to laugh but he didn't want to do it openly. He laughed to himself and cheered up at the thought that he hadn't had the slightest intention of answering back, much less starting the commotion. They were coming into the city. The bus's slow progress gave him time to read the huge billboard at the city's entrance: CITY OF LA CEIBA, FOUNDED IN 1877, POPULATION 50,000, a smudgy number, then, FEET ABOVE SEA LEVEL. The American hadn't opened his mouth again except to spit or moan in pain. *John, John, where are you?* It was the voice of the old woman sitting next to the American. She rubbed her eyes to finish waking up, *What's happened to you, my boy?* And starting to get up, she turned to him, *¿Qué le pasó a mi John?* The man in the suit answered, *Nothing, just a slight accident.* The old woman stroked the American's head and said, *Si él dice cosas no le hagan caso, mi boy estar enfermo de la cabeza.* All the passengers were quiet for a minute. They exchanged looks of surprise and smiles full of mischief. And again the voices rose in the bus, *Yes, but why did you fall asleep and leave the gringo unwatched knowing he wasn't right in the head? I'm so sorry, I didn't know it before or else I wouldn't have laughed so much. Thanks to him the trip was a lot of fun. It would be great if we always had along a gringo with such a good sense of humor, like our friend here.* And there was laughter all around.

Guillermo was saying nothing; his grandfather was smiling. They were facing each other. The grandson lay in a hammock, and the old man sat on some pieces of cardboard he had spread out on the floor. Every now and then the mouse peered from behind the beam; it looked on, its eyes flitting from place to place, almost like an insolent child. The grandfather emptied a palmful of tobacco into his pipe and lit it. Guillermo examined the cabin's four walls. As each minute passed, he grew more convinced that his grandfather would be a good character for his novel and the setting of the cabin spectacular and easy to describe. There was nothing to it, he thought, describing the cabin would be as easy as drinking a glass of water. Maybe he could embroider a little, for instance small details like the mouse or the cockroach that just then was climbing slowly up the wall; now it disappeared into a crack, reappeared higher up, then dropped to the ground and persisted all over again. *That's how persevering I'll have to be with my novel,* he told himself.

Leaning back on the floor, sucking on his pipe, his grandfather said:

"Go on with your story; and listen, didn't Chago write to you again?"

Guillermo, who for a good while had been holding on to the folder he always carried full of papers, looked for what his grandfather wanted:

"It must be in here."

His grandfather smiled:

"If I was you I'd know all that stuff by heart."

"It's not so easy."

Dear Guillermín:

How's it going ballbuster? I hope you're in good shape. I got your sheet of paper and I'll solve things for you little by little but before going on to anything else I want you to tell old man Chon and Luyi where the fuck to get off. What's with them anyway? Tell them to stop knocking my words.

So Fabian and Lelo took off for Olancho, huh? What a couple of freaks—with all that crap about the Red Book they can suck in a whole bunch of stupid guys up around there. You say the army's recruiting a helluva lot of guys? Well, don't get nervous, it's happening all over; the manhunters are also

operating around here, but I don't see why
all the shit now, since Somoza's washed up
in Nicaragua and it was him the guerrillas
were fighting against. Well, that's a horse
of a different color, but what I can tell
you is that Somoza got the fuck out a good
while ago and the songs of the revolution
are still popular around here. By the way,
the American woman I told you about is
still going with me. The poor thing be-
lieves the crap about the Latin lover. Us
students from the provinces who live here
in the capital know that what's in right
now is the Latin dollar. About the Honduran
chick I mentioned in my last letter, well I
hate to tell you but she stopped being my
girl one day suddenly. She caught me flat-
footed; I wasn't expecting it. So you see
she stopped being my girl, now she's my
woman. She was a virgin, only she's wild
about riding bikes and well, my innertube
provoked an accident, which is understand-
able. Nobody else had gotten into her.
(Maybe you can use this in your novel?)
It's taken me a long time to answer you but
after all you're the writer, you can't expect me to write too often. How did you
spend your Christmas and New Year's? Me, I
had a ball. I was at my uncle's place for
awhile and then I skipped out because I had

a date with a chick, a <u>piba</u>, like a friend
from Argentina at the U says. And I took
off with her and, you won't believe this, I
had a few beers, and after a good time on
the town I brought her to my room and the
<u>piba</u>, as the man says, was out of this
world. She stripped all the way and believe
it or not I was ashamed to strip down. I
couldn't get my rod up. I went into the
bathroom and I started whacking it but it
wouldn't get hard. I was worried. <u>This
can't be</u>, I said, <u>I'm turning into a fairy</u>.
But get this: I went back to bed and told
the chick I was sorry but I couldn't, and
she took a good look and started working
some black magic on me and, before you knew
it, it was up and ready for the charge. I
won't go on because if I do, you'll start
jacking off.

So you met a poet. I'm really glad for
you. You have to show him things you've
written and if they're not good, do them
over again. This writing bit is motherfuck-
ing hard and I don't know why but I'm bet-
ting on you.

I wish you could come here. You'd have
one helluva good time, because at this U
there's more women than you can shake a
stick at and most of them have a modus
vivendi (is that how you say it?). And they

prefer us, because the sons of the rich are
real prissy. And even if a girl goes with
one of them for his money you can take her
on as a lover and the rich motherfucker
will slip her bread to spend on you. See
the way we run things here? We're good
friends and I don't believe you'll consider
me a pimp. No, it's very simple, most of
the time we don't have a cent, and as students our only way out is the Latin dollar
or some girl with a spoiled mama's-and-pa-
pa's son for a boyfriend, get me?

You say you and Idalia came to a sad
ending, but Guillermo, what's wrong with
you? You've got to get her back. There are
damn few women like her around. I told you
I could go for her, and if you don't wise
up, I'm coming back for her. (I'm just kidding, man, don't go taking me seriously.)
Go ahead and get her back, she's a great
woman. You still have time. Further down in
your letter you ask me to describe El Porvenir, there you really shoved it to me all
the way, pal. What can I tell you about the
place? The truth is, I don't know. El Porvenir is like something there isn't much to
tell about. Its unpaved streets are swollen
with weeds at the edges, streets that are
empty most of the time anyway. In fact I
don't know what to tell you. Maybe if you

hadn't asked me right out, I could've come
up with something, but what the hell. So
we'll let it go 'til another time. I'd
rather tell you about something that happened to me there.

Look, before the Army grabbed me, I was
walking near the plantation clinic when,
near me, I noticed a fuckin' girl I'd never
seen before, and she wasn't bad to look at.
So I started softening her up a little and
she told me she had come to El Porvenir the
day before but wasn't from there. I asked
her if I could walk along with her, and she
said sure. I suggested that we follow the
railroad tracks, but shit, she said no. She
knew she wouldn't stand a chance there, so
we went down the street. We passed a
pineapple field that had been harvested.
She said she liked to look at the fields
when they were all green but not like this
one. It already looked kind of yellow. We
reached town, she said it was such a lonely
place, I didn't want to tell her the weird
habit people have here, of everybody spying
on you when you go past, spying on you
through cracks or partly open doors. Up
until then I hadn't tried out my line, I
just listened to her, because she kept com-
plaining that most of the houses in El Porvenir were built of wood or mud. She had

only seen one made of cement. And she
moaned that pigs and cows shouldn't run
loose in the streets, streets were for people to walk in, and that it was so hot in
this damn town. I asked her if she knew it
well. She said no, so I took her to the
town hall. Why did I take her there? She
really shot her mouth off there. She actually had to ask me if that soccer field
full of potholes and horse and cow shit was
the center of town. How awful it was to
have to reveal that the town hall and the
church were the beginning and the end of El
Porvenir. If she were the mayor or mayoress
(I'm not sure how to say it) by now she'd
have had them cut down all the bushes that
blocked her view of the church and she'd
have stopped the cows from crossing the
soccer field, and she'd have all those pot-
bellied kids without any shirts dress like
decent people. I told her let's go on walking, maybe she'd like the beach. We went
there, I asked her if she wanted to go for
a swim, she said she'd like to but those
beaches were so filthy that they turned her
off, and besides she wasn't wearing a
bathing suit. It took me half an hour to
convince her the beaches were always deserted and she could perfectly well bathe
in her panties. And that's how it was, she

took off her skirt and said she didn't want
to wet her bra. You should've seen her
well-built chassis. I grabbed hold of her
in no time flat and we rolled all over the
sand. And I'm telling you, not Columbus,
not Francis de las Casas nor any conquista-
dor ever fucked an Indian woman like I
fucked her and without even having to talk
her into it. What a bunch of shit. Everything I've just said is a lie. I did it to
see if I could help you describe El Porvenir. At least I tried, and if I go on
like this, I think you and me both will
sign the novel.

There's nothing new going on here in
Teguci. Not even witches go out at night.
And there on the plantation, anything going
on? The other day I was thinking about your
novel, and I'll give you another little
piece of help, on condition that we share
author's rights, OK? Look, since the novel
will be about the plantation I already have
the title. Make it Return to the
Plantation. How's that sound? You know why
I say that title would suit it to a T? Because working there is like being in a con-
centration camp, shit! My blood freezes
over when I remember it, and if there's one
thing I wouldn't want in this life, it's
exactly that, to return to the plantation.

OK, I've been pushing this pen long
enough. My fingers already ache. I seldom
write as much horseshit as this. Tell old
Chon and old Luyi that I haven't written
them each a letter because stamps cost too
much, but this one is for them too. Ok
dude, 'til next time, best,

Chago

"What a rascal," the grandfather said, laughing.
Guillermo took a drink of water:
"You should meet Chago."
Before talking, his grandfather sucked on his pipe:
"With what I've heard, I feel as if I already know
him."
He came to his feet, lit the oil lamp, mentioned that
it was getting dark out. Guillermo was carefully running
his eyes over the four walls and couldn't rid his mind of
the idea that his grandfather would be a character in his
novel, even though he lived far away from the plantation. His problem now was how to get him in, since
there was nothing to connect the mountain with the
plantation. He smiled, thinking of the poet's advice,
You must write about reality with imagination.
His grandfather leaned back again to let him know
that he was ready to go on listening. The mouse turned
up once more and became absorbed watching the light
from the oil lamp.

Like this man—whether I feel sorry for him or he makes me happy I don't know—who affects me deeply when I discover that there are people like him. And as always, Beti, I went to your house and spilled the whole story: Did you see the paper? Look, there was a news story about a man they found dead in a place a long way from the city. He was all disfigured and, apart from his relatives, I don't think anyone would have recognized his face. The official version is that they attacked him with robbery in mind or that perhaps a personal enemy murdered him. But his family came up with a scrap of paper—from a pack of cigarettes— the dead man carried in one of his shoes. On it was written: "From Marcos to Carmen. I am a prisoner in a police cell." Don't you see? Beti looks at me and laughs. She's not laughing with me, she's laughing with her brain. A person and his or her brain make a perfect duo. Beti is laughing at what is passing through her mind, and who can guess what that might be? No one. What passes through her head is hers. Perhaps a clown passes through, or some character she finds funny, or chances are it's the Law passing through and this makes her laugh. The laughter they hate, the common weapon that strikes deep. Laughter, excellent invention, destroyer, builder, challenger. I love laughter because it's like loving the only weapon we have left. Beti is splitting her side laughing as she hasn't done in ages. I laugh too, thanks to what we're thinking about.

17

The days were slipping by and Guillermo was still undecided about going to see Idalia. He thought about the poet's words of advice, about Chon's and Luyi's, but no, he still wasn't ready to come to a decision. On Saturday he swore he would go, even if he had to visit a drugstore first and buy himself some tranquilizers, which was what he did, in a way. The drugstore—his name for the bar—was jumping with Saturday euphoria and it was still early in the afternoon, *maybe two o'clock,* he said to himself. The sun was beating down hard and he was soaked to the skin in sweat when he walked in. The waitress came over and before she could ask, he ordered, *a beer,* with the air of an old boozer. The waitress returned fast and perhaps for the first time in his life he didn't notice her low neckline or her dress or anything. The juke box was screaming its head off, *youuuuuu come to meeeeee now that I'm leeeeaving,* and he thought of his friend the professor who had told him that Charles Chaplin composed it for a sweetheart. *It must have been the first time Chaplin didn't make anybody laugh,* he murmured. The next beer went down as fast as the first and he raised his hand in the well-known signal that he wanted another of the same. At some other tables couples were drinking, necking, and exchanging smiles. Guillermo was feeling envy and counting the hours till he too would have his girl beside him. The bar continued to fill up with couples and single drinkers. Some customers, very drunk by now, were talking in shouts about the country's next president; others were discussing the National Soccer Team's extraordinary victory only a few days before. A woman with too much makeup on came over to the table, *Why so alone, my prince?* He tipped his half-finished beer to his lips until there wasn't a drop left. *In the first place I'm not alone, and in the second place I'm not a prince. I don't know who gave you permission to lower my status.* The woman looked all around her to see who was with him. He laughed *I'm not alone, because you're with me and I'm not a prince because I'm Reynaldo, Rey (King) for short.* The woman burst out laughing *Oh this Rey is so funny* and she stroked his chin. Guillermo raised his left hand, making the V for victory and the waitress knew it meant two beers but yelled *Twooo?* from where she was. He nodded first and then shook his head. The woman with the painted face, who was now sitting across from him, said *What a stupid waitress* and the juke box screamed *To go on living, I need to forget.* And now he was about to tell the woman to shut her trap because he had to listen to the song in silence. It was the one Idalia liked to hum. The painted woman apparently understood. She kept quiet, drinking her beer and glancing from one table to the next. *Our dream was over, when our love ended like the evening, wasting away.* Guillermo drained his beer, dragged steadily on his cigarette, and the woman, *Rey, if you keep on drinking so fast you won't even be able to stand up.* He stared at her as if demanding who had asked for her precious opinion. *Sometimes I want to break out laughing,* and the woman seemed to be hearing something behind the music, while he remained absorbed, listening. The bar kept filling up, the waitress passed very close to Guillermo and said in his ear, *Watch out, she's a hustler, she'll clean you out.* The painted woman caught on and got up, saying something like *This bitch is just jealous.* His song had ended and he decided to leave. In the street he could hear music sprouting everywhere. La Ceibans went past in their regular groups of five to ten persons, with towels and hats, cassette players going full blast. This gave him the idea to continue drinking at the beach. Without thinking twice, he stopped a cab—as he always did on payday—and with a couple of signs from him the driver knew where to go. At the beach people were having more fun than anywhere else. Girls in bathing suits were running all over the sand. From a large thatch-roofed music shed full of blacks Guillermo watched everything. The female bodies made him forget his cares. One especially, a girl in a yellow bathing suit with her back to him. He was getting ready to go make a play for her, repeating popular sayings to himself like *Fight fire with fire* or *New loves forget old loves,* but he couldn't get up the nerve; he thought of Idalia. If she suddenly turned up and found him with another girl it would be the grand finale. Then he asked himself, what would Idalia be doing in one of these places? What's more, the girl in the yellow bathing suit was good enough to eat, and she seemed so alone that he and no one else seemed able to rescue her. There was no longer any doubt in his mind. He headed for her, and he had only gone two steps when a guy came up to her with two glasses in his hands.

Anyway, he didn't stop. He'd have to be satisfied with seeing her close up, winking at her. And perhaps next time he'd be the one laughing with her the way she was laughing now with her companion. The girl looked behind her, Guillermo got such a shock he almost keeled over. Why hadn't he recognized her before? It was Idalia herself—in bathing suit and soul—who was also watching him with fear in her eyes. At that moment there were a thousand things he wanted to do but the hard guy with her was bigger than him. He didn't want to make an ass of himself. He felt more jealous than ever. He stopped dead, then returned to the shed, thinking it wasn't the right time to settle accounts with the thief who had robbed him of his love. He went on drinking with no thought for himself. The shed was jumping, the blacks were drinking, dancing, and singing. A gorgeous black woman came over and held out her hand, inviting him to dance. He accepted and everyone formed a circle, bobbing up and down to the rhythm of two drums.

One of the drummers had hair that was completely white and made his face look blacker than it actually was. Guillermo let out a horse-laugh when the black woman dancing with him said in his ear that the white-haired black's nickname was *Negative*. The minutes passed and with the place jumping more and more, Guillermo forgot his desire for vengeance. The black woman had him in her power. She would move in, swivelling her enormous hips very fast. The grinding movement fascinated him and he kept telling her not to stop. He already had a hard-on, and his every thought was telling him that tonight he would make black love. Bottles passed from hand to hand. Guillermo, who had vowed not to drink rum because it was too powerful, forgot his promise and tipped the bottle to his lips. The liquor scraped his throat. He felt that he was burning up. His whole chest seemed to be on fire. The black woman stuck to him like gum. She followed him wherever he went.

He was so far gone that he couldn't walk straight. In his drunken state, he got the idea of going to the bathroom. He knew the black woman would string along. The bathroom was a good way from the shed. He pretended to make a mistake and, instead of going into the john, he stepped into the shower room. The black woman went in to get him out, *The toilet is on the other side.* He laughed *But I feel like taking a shower.* She also laughed *No, let's go back to the shed, stop acting crazy* and she went over to drag him out. It's what he was waiting for and, without giving her a chance to slip away, he gripped her shoulders hard. The woman rocked, she did her best to break free but couldn't, the hands possessing her were two tongs. In spite of her insults, threats, and whines, he kept trying to kiss her. She tried to scratch him. He managed to kiss her and held his lips glued to hers for six minutes. All she did was keep up a soft *nooooo* with low moans in between, a no that said the opposite, a no that let him squeeze her breasts and go after something under her skirt, a no that made them shudder together naked, standing up, leaning against the wall. Her last audible words were gentle, persuasive *I thought all Indians had a small one.*

An hour later he was still drinking beer in the shed when he suddenly saw the girl in the yellow swimsuit come in with the big stud. He stood up with his bottle in his hand, went over to them, *Idalia, don't you remember me?* The girl looked surprised, *Are you talking to me? I'm not Idalia.* He was reeling. The girl's face seemed more and more familiar to him and, still holding on to the bottle, he turned to the hard guy *And you, what are you doing with Idalia?* The man turned pale. He brought his hand up to his mouth and, biting the nail of his pinky, *We're not bothering you, leave us alone, my sister's name is not Idalia, who knows what Idalia you're getting her mixed up with.* He spoke in a high-pitched voice that made Guillermo want to laugh but he checked himself. In the same effeminate inflection the man went on, *We can be friends if you like, but no rough stuff, see? If I were you, I'd go look for Idalia at her home.* Guillermo shook his head. He remembered that it was exactly where he was headed. He saw that the girl in the yellow bathing suit only resembled Idalia a little. He decided to have a few more beers to build up the courage to go to his lost love.

18

He opened his eyes. He looked all around him as if he were lost. The morning sun came in right through the curtains. Everything looked strange. His mind was a sea of incoherent thoughts. The sofa on which he lay was dark, as dark as his brain. He asked himself *Where am I? Who brought me here?* No one answered him, only his stomach, growling like an animal poised to attack. He understood absolutely nothing. He got up without making noise, got as far as the wall, his eyes like a thief's. Then he saw her watching him accusingly; he went over to her. The face looked familiar. *Those eyes, that expression.* He stared at the photograph. *I know this face.* The sound of a door startled him, *In that photo Idalia was only fourteen,* the voice he'd heard behind him turned into a gentle smile. Guillermo had swung around, *Good morning, ma'am.* Only then did he start to understand his presence here more clearly. He recalled yesterday's drunken spree. Images came to him like picture postcards: *beers in the drugstore, woman with painted face, to forget I need to live, waitress coming and going, taxi taking me to the beach, girl in yellow bathing suit, shed with blacks, Idalia and him* (not Guillermo, but the other one), *beer in a glass, and you what's wrong with you? beach and ocean, Idalia you don't remember me, angry big guy, I'm not Idalia, naked black woman, nails scratching him, breasts, bottle of rum, open legs, shed, blacks, shed with blacks, blacks in shed, beers beer bee be b* . . . The lady held out a towel and pointed to the bathroom. He didn't know whether to act as if nothing had happened or get out of there as fast as he could. Idalia's mother told him that breakfast would soon be ready, to sit in the dining room and wait.

He was puzzled. Idalia's mother was treating him as if nothing had happened. He knew himself very well, and even if he couldn't remember what he had really done, he suspected that there had been nothing good about it, either for his reputation or for his recovery of Idalia. He felt cold, his stomach was telling him that it wouldn't be able to keep anything down except an ice-cold beer, but now he felt it was his duty not to refuse the breakfast Idalia's mother was offering him, even if he had to make a hundred tries. The day after he had hung a big one on, he never ate or got up this early. Besides he wasn't used to waking up anywhere except at home. He thought he'd better leave. His mother must be very worried, imagining that the Army had picked him up. Idalia's mother didn't give him any more time to think of deserting. She served breakfast for two. She told him *Eat a lot and don't be shy, make yourself at home.* He thanked her in a low voice.

Idalia's mother sat down across from him, watched him out of the corner of her eye and felt compassion for the poor stray sheep, the tender sheep that had run away from its shepherd. Precious sheep that some day not far off—before the coming of Armageddon—would have to return to the good path and promise never to wander again to the edge of the thornbushes. She went on with her monologue, looking for possible snares to bring the stray within the circle of salvation.

The sheep was munching slowly. The food went down his throat only because he forced it down. He ate without raising his eyes, without haste. From time to time he would throw a look at the refrigerator. He knew that's where the medicine needed to restore him was. He imagined the bottle of almost frozen water, delicious to tip into his mouth and not stop till the last drop was gone. Idalia's mother felt happy submitting herself to the divine ordeal. It seemed to her that she already had one foot—and part of the other—in Heaven. Enduring all the things that Guillermo had put her through the night before was proof of the great provocation Lucifer had concocted to provoke her. But she had resisted all temptation. She hadn't become angry, not for a minute. She had spoken no word against her neighbor. Her faith had not wavered, not for a second. He could hear the sounds of people rising all over the house. Guillermo's heart was puffing up like a balloon. He took a guess at everything he heard: the loud rasp of someone spitting out a lunger, the steady scrub of someone brushing his teeth, the sharp sound of someone lifting the lid of a toilet seat; silence and footsteps, the sign that someone had forgotten the toilet roll, steps coming back and silence; a woman urinating or was it a man pissing expertly against the walls of the bowl without making any noise at all? While Idalia's mother kept her eyes on Guillermo as if he were her property, he was slowly dying of anticipation of the next meaningful sound that would let him know if it was Idalia or her father who had gotten up. The sound of someone ripping cardboard calmed him; in the left side of his chest the balloon started to lose air; the dates coincided; he grew happy, totally convinced that Idalia was having her period. No one on earth could have persuaded him—no matter how hard they tried—that the ripped cardboard wasn't the top of a box of sanitary napkins flying into the nearest wastepaper basket.

Idalia's mother still kept her eyes on his face. He was

putting on an act. He was chewing his food more than was normal. He watched his cup of coffee like the enemy he had never had. The mother's eyes went right through his. At this point, he thought, she already knows the shape of my brain, my facial bone structure, the sides of my scalp, all the components of my throat, the size of my intestines, my liver which is about to rebel, my blood vessels, the sacs of my testicles; he stopped thinking. He told himself things weren't really that bad; she was staring at him but perhaps not directly into his eyes. A door, whose hinges needed oil, opened. He restrained his neck with all his might to stop it from veering to the right. A *Good morning* exploded in his ears; he didn't hear himself answer with a weak, submissive *How are you?* Her voice kept coming closer, *How did you sleep, mama? Is my breakfast ready?* And she stood before him, only her voice, because he didn't dare raise up his head to discover anything else. The voice didn't sound again but its source was there in front of him, and he wanted it to speak till it made him deaf. The voice needed only his provocation to continue; he let out two small, cautionary, intentional coughs: *And how are you, Idalia?* and lifted his eyes like an actor in a TV detective series. She smiled—he knew she wasn't smiling at him—and after a pause prepared with premeditation, treachery, and advantage, *I believe I should be the one asking that question, don't you think?* He heard nothing, and he didn't want to hear. One side of his chest was an outburst of fireworks that burned all the way down to his toenails. She had embraced him with her eyes like before, and in the next five minutes that embrace would make his hangover and its effects disappear completely forever. This was the old Idalia, the one with the surprising answers and the bedroom eyes. Here she was with only a table separating them, as if with a saw he could cut through its thickness and rescue her from that awful distance. Her mother returned to serve breakfast, sure that her prayers had reached Heaven because she saw that the stray sheep—pale, without an appetite, sleepless a few minutes before—was now all color, purity, avid for breakfasts and coffees, eyes with sparks of divine illumination. The mother took a moment to give thanks for having been heard; she was grateful and congratulated herself for being the one who had delivered the stray sheep to safety. The three ate in silence, passing the salt, reaching for the tortillas, offering more sugar, refusing butter, hands touching accidentally, eyes meeting, letting the coffee flow down their throats, praising the meat, attacking the chili pepper, apologizing for spilling things, ignoring the lettuce, and hands touching accidentally again, smiles, and questions and laughter. *What's the matter?* They look at the mother whose entire body is brimming over with happiness. *Nothing, Guillermo, it's just that you make me laugh,* and another splurge of laughter. *But I haven't said anything funny, have I?* Mother and daughter understand each other, and this time he wished he could put the gentle voice before a firing squad, *It's because of last night,* and he feels his life stretching like rubber into the living room, through the hallway, out on the street. Mother watches her sheep redden, pretends not to see this for two seconds but can't hold back at the third. Intuitively Guillermo hits upon the best way out and joins them with a forced laugh. Deep down he'd like to take Idalia by the hair and sweep the house with her, teach her to be discreet. Idalia is perfectly familiar with her guest's reactions and to forestall a disastrous ending, she puts on an act with a *It's all over and done with,* and invents more hunger on her part. Mother gets up and leaves them to themselves. Guillermo doesn't intend to miss his chance and, glancing around him, he goes over to Idalia and lifts her face; he returns to his place after giving her a kiss so short that it was more like something disposable. Without giving her time to catch her breath, he suggested that they go out the following week. She preferred to make the date that same night. He said yes. Sadness settled over him when he remembered the cardboard top of the sanitary napkins and he began to resign himself. *You don't have to worry, everything's okay.* When he heard this his erection came to him special delivery and he wondered how much time there was before nightfall. He felt in his pockets. He tried to remember names of people who might lend him money, or things he might hock or sell. Idalia guessed and, with half a smile, *I don't have any money today, Guillermo.* And he grows red by stages: first he's completely pale, then red, and immediately pink. *It's not that bad,* Idalia comes back at him, and he feels red inside and out. *I can lend you something,* she says without looking up. His natural color returns and he decides he's not going to turn down the offer, not even for the sake of politeness. He feels like posing in front of a mirror and letting both the Guillermo inside and the one outside the mirror split their sides laughing. Idalia has a hunch that he's laughing inside. *What's up? What's so funny?* He makes believe he's thinking for a couple of seconds, *It's because of last night, it's because of last night.* And she pretends to believe him and he pretends to believe that she has believed him and they laugh just for the hell of it. Mother comes back, Bible in hand. Guillermo feels himself scorching in eternal fire. And Idalia helps him make his escape, *Mama, Guillermo has to go now, his mother must be desperate.* And he agrees so as to leave no room for doubt and says goodbye to Idalia and to her mother who is there with the Bible wide open. And she says, *Come back with more time, there are things here that you have to learn.* Guillermo goes down the street as excited as a schoolboy who's up to some mischief, repeating, over and over, that he's the only one in the world who can change color whenever it's convenient and that had he been born near Hollywood or Broadway, his would be a different future.

This is getting more and more damned tough since they banned thinking about certain things, about peace, for instance. And what I say is, I was never interested in thinking about peace till the censor came along. I went running to your house, Beti, and I whispered in your ear: Have you heard about the new law? It is absolutely forbidden to think about peace. And you laughed, laughed and laughed and, still laughing, you said: It never entered my head to think about it. And from then on we couldn't shake off the curiosity to meditate on peace and went off to investigate it. I tried for hours on end to personify peace. What was it like? Lean? Fat? Smiling? White? Simple? Friendly? And so question followed question. Peace, the absence of war. Peace, to sleep under a roof. Peace, not to go hungry. Peace, not to be afraid. Peace, to go out and be almost sure that you're coming back alive. Peace, work. Peace, harmony. Peace, school. Peace, health. Peace, peace. And peace stayed in my head for a long time. And later they banned thinking about the word escape. No one was to talk about, let alone imagine, ways of escaping. Flight was eliminated from the dictionary, flight no one could carry out, ultimate defection. Beti and I decided not to think of escaping but to escape to think about escaping. And we ran away from the country, the earth, the galaxy for several hours.

19

"Today it's hot enough to make strong men melt," Chon said, looking at the sun.

"How about dropping in on the poet after work today?" Guillermo suggested.

"It's a good idea," Chon decided.

"Fine by me," Luyi said.

"We'll go to the poet's," Chon spoke again, smiling, "that is if the sun hasn't dissolved us by then."

"I hope the sun melts the Company," Guillermo commented, putting an unlit cigarette in his mouth.

"None for me?" Luyi asked.

"For everybody," Guillermo answered and held out the pack.

"The Company's leaving and La Ceiba'll sink into the sea," Chon said without interrupting his chewing.

Guillermo dragged on his cigarette; he ran his eyes over his feet and then on to the horizon where the plantation disappeared:

"It won't leave, it'll never leave on its own, if it leaves some day it'll be because we kicked it out."

"It can't leave," Luyi agreed.

"The Union can save us," Chon said.

Guillermo sat down, forming a triangle with Chon and Luyi; he leaned forward and tried to blow smoke rings.

"The Union save us?" was all he said.

Chon undid the knots on the cloth that covered his lunch pail; he held up the thermos bottle:

"There's still some coffee here for anybody who wants it."

"I do. They say it's a good refresher."

"Count me in too," Guillermo said with a steady smile.

He and Luyi unpacked the bags that carried their lunches. Chon uncovered his food and suggested:

"How about us dividing up our stuff? I've brought plenty of cheese."

"You read my mind."

One passed cheese to another, the third received chopped meat and in return gave fried ripe plantain. The butter went around the triangle, the tortillas were shared equally. When they all had some of everything Chon said:

"See, this way we all eat well."

"So long as you don't give us any tobacco," Guillermo said.

They were chewing and laughing under their hats. The huge plantation didn't have a single shade tree to shield them from the sun. While he ate, Chon said:

"I notice you're very happy. What's up?"

"There's no reason to be sad."

Luyi grinned:

"A few days ago you weren't saying that."

"It's the heat. I like heat."

Both old men burst out laughing:

"The heat from a pair of buttocks, or some other heat?"

"Because the sun doesn't have an ass," Luyi said.

The old men went into their horse-laugh again. Trying to make the conversation take a serious turn, Guillermo said:

"Don't laugh, it's just that my girl has me in a happy mood."

"Aha, isn't that what we said before? Is she yours or are you getting her hot for somebody else?"

The three broke out laughing. Chon insisted:

"Well, aren't you going to tell us why you're so happy?"

"No, it's nothing."

Luyi stopped chewing:

"Tell us, man. After all, talking about it is what makes it fun."

"You'll find out soon enough."

The old men laughed. It was time to go into the fields:

"We only have to put up with this fucking sun a bit longer today," Chon said.

"Afterwards we'll go to the poet's, right?" Guillermo added.

They sat down. Chon protested about the heat, the dust and the salary. The poet agreed with their gripes and said there was too much injustice. Luyi took off his hat, ran a hand through his white hair, let his back collapse against the wall and, in the middle of a yawn, he backed up Chon's complaints with *This life is shit.* Guillermo took out a comb and, posing in front of a yellowish mirror with broken corners, said *Pure shit, all of it. Some day this country'll have to change.*

"By that time I'll be in my grave," Chon said.

"We'll all be, but maybe not Guillermo," Luyi said.

"In this business of death nobody knows who'll be the first to buy his ticket.

The poet laughed and Guillermo thought himself the cleverest person in the galaxy. He told himself that drawing a laugh or tears from a poet could only be done by an equal, like himself, López Guillermo, who was already starting to give the country's literary critics something to talk about.

"Some guy, this Guillermo," Chon said, turning to the poet, "the fucker's happier than ever today. And he claims it's the heat. What do you make of that, poet? The only heat makes anybody happy is the heat from a pair of buttocks, or don't you agree, poet?"

The poet's laughter sounded like a stampede and Guillermo felt that he was being deposed from the throne of his cleverness. Before anyone could worsen his position further, he said:

"A pair of incendiary buttocks."

And laughter spilled from the mouths of all and flowed into Guillermo's ears like a symphony not even Mozart could have improved.

"Yes," the poet said with a cough that Guillermo believed was just an act, "I think it's the heat that makes him so happy, right?"

During the riot of laughter Guillermo defended himself:

"Well, could be, but it's personal."

"Just tell us how many times you shot your load."

"Junior here can't shoot more than once or twice."

"Don't you believe it," Guillermo, who had been touched where he lived, answered, "I've done it eight times in one night."

The hearty laughter of the two old men and the poet filled the whole waiting room:

"Not even if you were a *burro*."

"One shot is the most you can manage and you come out saying eight, where?"

No, I believe him: Guillermo is too serious to lie. Besides, I think the right thing would be to ask the girl, so who is she?"

"Hi, everybody; I see you're having a grand time."

The laughs turned into a dreadful silence. Guillermo felt like the biggest pervert in the world; the voice that had come in through the door had left him numb.

"Come in," the poet said.

"Thanks, but I'm already in, so why don't you tell me the joke?"

Guillermo felt as if they had just pumped a quart of seriousness into his veins; the old men and the poet were laughing to themselves:

"No, Idalia; we were laughing at Standard. They think that if it leaves we'll be sunk, and the poet says the only thing that is going to sink are the ships loaded with pineapples."

"Good joke," she said with a smile, "but not good enough for all the laughing you could hear a kilometer away.

"No," Chon came to the rescue, "we were telling jokes ladies shouldn't hear."

"That's right," Luyi said.

"And what can I do for you?"

Idalia drew a vial from her bag:

"I'd like you to give me this shot."

The poet stood up. He took the vial and went in through a door marked *Injection Room,* asking Idalia to follow him.

When the door closed Guillermo wanted to shout after the poet to give her the shot in the arm. He imagined Idalia lying on her stomach, exposing those beauties that were for his eyes only. The five minutes she was in there seemed to last forever and more than once he thought of rapping on the door. And then and there he realized how deeply in love and how extremely jealous of everyone he was. With the poet following, Idalia limped over to sit with the rest of the group; Chon and Luyi were talking softly, as if they were plotting something; Guillermo was twisting his face in pain, in empathy with Idalia.

"I believe one is enough," the poet said.

Looking curious, Luyi asked:

"What does she have?"

"Cold symptoms; but I'll soon get over it."

"Medicine in time will break any cold," Chon said.

"That's right," the poet added, "prevention is better than cure."

After thinking for a few minutes, Guillermo said:

"How are things going in the Union?"

Everyone was interested in what Idalia would answer:

"From bad to worse; Standard is threatening to leave."

"But why?"

"They say they're losing money, that the workers' strikes and demands are going to make them go bankrupt, and that the Honduran worker is worthless."

Chon, who had just carried a chunk of tobacco to his mouth, protested:

"Let them stop that fuckin' shit. What about the beating we take from morning till night? They just want to fuck us up."

"That's capitalism," the poet commented, "Invest less and draw bigger profits. The Company can't leave because it's making millions here; threatening to leave is their way of keeping the workers down."

"What pisses me off," added Chon, "is that shit about the worker being lazy."

"This," the poet explained, "is easy to see. From our ancestors we have testimonies that we have always been hard workers. But with the coming of the Spanish Conquest everything changed. They took over our traditions, beliefs, riches, our land. According to history, our Indians didn't want masters. They preferred being killed to becoming slaves. You might say that unconsciously they started strikes, the kind we call a sit-down strike. And from those times we've inherited our rebellious spirit toward masters; we're not lazy but defenders of our rights."

Luyi, whose arms were folded against his chest, nodded his agreement:

"It's something I never thought about before."

"That's why it's good," Chon said, "to talk to educated persons, because they teach you a lot."

"Things are going to get tougher now," Idalia said. "Standard won't leave. It'll stay on like it always does. But the workers are going to form cooperatives and sell Standard the fruit."

"What about the workers' equipment, the machines? The workers don't have any of their own," the poet said.

Idalia looked shaken up when she answered:

"Standard will always own everything. It will rent them out to the workers."

"But won't that be bad for us?" Luyi asked.

"Sure. They'll fire permanent workers. They'll pay them off at reduced salary rates and there won't be any permanent workers. The workers won't get paid by the hour anymore, only for the amount of work they do, and there'll be days when they won't earn a cent."

Chon looked terribly frightened:

"Is all this true, Idalia? You're joking, aren't you?"

"No, I'm not joking; it's true. The Union is taking steps to keep this from happening but, who knows, there are rumors that Standard will make trouble for the Union."

"What'll become of us?" Guillermo said and stopped himself from saying any more.

"Are they going to let us all go?" Chon asked.

"That's right, all except the bosses; they'll always work with Standard and their salaries will go up. The rest of the workers lose all their rights: hospital, compensations, claims."

Clamping his jaws together and clenching his fists, Chon shouted:

"Fleas always stick to the skinniest dog. What am I going to do when cutting pineapples is all I know?"

"I knew all about it but I didn't want to say anything. This is my last month working here. I'll soon be off to try my luck somewhere else."

Guillermo felt the poet's words like a blow to his chest with a machete. He didn't see how the poet could possibly have thought of leaving without saying anything to him, his friend and colleague. Unable to hide his anger, he asked:

"Poet, how could you go away without saying goodbye to me?"

The poet smiled because he understood his resentment very well:

"There's still a month to go, Guillermo. We'll have time to talk, to say goodbye and maybe even go for walks and a few beers."

His eyes lit up and, in what seemed like a far away voice, he said:

"I'm sorry, poet."

Idalia laughed:

"Don't let this boy have too many beers, poet."

He blushed. Idalia's mother crossed his mind and, to change the subject, he pretended to be thirsty. Depressed by all the news, Chon had hung his head; Luyi was slapping him gently on the shoulder and muttering softly that everything in this life had a solution and that Standard would pay some day for all the damage done. The poet was whistling one of his favorite melodies, the adagio movement from an opera, as he always did when he had nothing to say. Idalia watched Guillermo step up to the tap, cupping his hands.

"All this has left us dumb," Luyi said.

The poet interrupted his whistling:

"That's it, we're in the dumbest country in the world."

I'm leaving," Chon said, getting to his feet, "I'm leaving. I've got to think about what I'll do after they kick me off this goddamn plantation."

The bitterness in Chon's face infected them all and one by one they agreed that it was time to go. They took leave of one another almost without a word. And from a window, the poet watched them going off, while he whistled his sad adagio.

Life is hard, boy, and I see it hasn't been easy for you. You've stopped talking, as if you were remembering the poet's sad adagio. Life hurts, but it hurts in some corners of the earth more than in others. And here I was, thinking you were the spirit of a dead man from somewhere far away; but no, you're blood of my blood and you came this far; if you were able to find your way to this dying old man that I am, you'll be able to find your way to everything in life. Tomorrow I'll get up early, tomorrow it's my turn to tell you why I left the city, let down by a woman, and how, by the time I had forgotten her, I had grown used to living here alone with my old dog who has since died. On a day like this, like all the days here, my dog didn't come as usual to scratch at the door, and I looked for him the way you look for your best friend, and found him lying still, still like everything that's not alive. I hugged him to me, crying, and I bawled the hell out of him for being disloyal, for dying first. You're like something Heaven has sent, now that I'm more alone than ever, and no longer know how to go back to the city to die among strangers. And people once said I was a man with a future, because being a grade school teacher in those days was like being a god in your neighborhood, one of the city's gods. And look at me here today with nothing to my name, dead in this life, dead and still walking after death, and half crazy sometimes, hearing voices without bodies. I hope you haven't come to stay in this place for good; I won't let you. You haven't even brought along a dog to keep you company for awhile. You can't stay because you've learned so much. Nowadays one learns more than we used to. Now young boys like to talk to us name-forgetting old men about life. You talk of everything we don't know. And you've got to go on telling me all there's left to tell, all that's been happening. I feel young again when I hear you talk. I feel that I'm flesh and blood, a dead man coming back to life; go on telling me, boy, don't stop, go on telling until night closes my eyes. Go on.

I'll try to tell you things that are not so sad, grandpa. I see you there lost in thought, eyes riveted on the wall, and maybe you're thinking about old man Chon who said goodbye to go off and cry along the road, without anyone seeing him, or about the poet's sad opera that Idalia and I could still hear quite a distance away. I don't want to see you thoughtful or sad, grandpa; I want you to laugh at the good and the bad things I'm telling. I want you to know that if I came to this place of solitude where nobody will disturb me, it's to write for about six months and go back, and so that you'll go with me and take your mouse with you if you don't want to leave it alone here. We have to make grandfathers laugh; I think somebody somewhere said that or maybe I'm the one who said it. And there's the rooster crowing again, grandpa; they say that roosters crow at eleven and at three in the morning, so it's eleven now, grandpa, eleven and your eyes are so open it looks like you're not going to sleep for a long while yet. I promise to put you in my novel, to make you a character that no one will forget, and also your mouse that I suppose amuses you when I'm not here. It clowns around and maybe you laugh and throw a stone at it but only to shoo it off, you'd never kill it; not for anything in the world would you want to harm it; it would be like hurting yourself—you'd both die at the same moment, the mouse looking at you as if it were asking you why you did it, and you lying on the floor, using your last breath to watch it with your eyes, telling it to forgive you, that you were only playing with it, that your blurry vision caused the accident—both of you dying together as in a game. Now you're watching me, grandpa; you watch me as if asking for more, to go on, never to stop. You don't need the serenades of insects and night birds anymore, you know them by heart.

20

A week later, the president of the Union had disappeared as if by magic. From what Idalia told me, they'd been planning a strike to make Standard pay all arrears in salary to the hundreds of workers dismissed. Two days before the strike was set to begin, they picked up the president. People who saw it said he was walking home when a white car without license plates pulled up beside him. Three men wearing ski masks and armed with machine guns ordered him to get in; he asked what for and the answer obtained was a flurry of fists and gun butts. More than thirty hours had passed since the abduction when she told me this, and there was still no news of him; the strike couldn't get under way. I felt terrible about the *compañero*. I knew what a big risk he had taken. Chances were they wouldn't ever find him and, you know, my girl to some extent was also part of the Union leadership. And that scared the hell out of me. If I ran into someone we both knew, the first thing I expected him to say was that she was also disappeared. It's rough . . . fucking rough. You feel nauseated and your balls feel ready to drop off . . . You remember what people say or what's in the papers. You're frightened, scared shitless. You start asking yourself things. You don't know what will be next. It's horrible...They never find you or else they do...but you're not the same. You're skin and bones, you can't walk or you're wandering on your feet, like a madman. That's if you're a man, but think of a woman...Chances are the first thing they do is strip her naked, satisfy themselves on her—not one guy only, but every one of them. You picture your girl naked, putting up a fight, bleeding, screaming your name, trying to save herself any way she can, but in the end she has to give in and you can almost see those filthy hands squeeze her breasts, force her legs open savagely. You can almost see the bastards start to kiss the lips she shares only with you and you feel scared. You imagine it's real, that it's the next one's turn and the next and the next and...then you can't stand thinking so you go out, wandering like a maniac...you go looking for her, afraid that what you've been thinking is true. You cross streets without watching out for the traffic lights. You jostle people who're in your way and you don't apologize; you feel the road getting longer...At last you come to her house, open the gate, forgetting that the dog may be off its leash... You call at the door, two seconds pass and no one opens, so you walk right in...When you're inside you don't see her in the living room and you want to shout her name...But just then she comes out of her room, you stare and stare at her again, looking her up and down to make sure it's her...When you hear her voice, so familiar to you, asking *What's wrong?*...you don't answer...you breathe once, only once but very deeply...You forget there may be others present...You rush over and throw your arms around her ...kiss her...when your voice returns you only tell her to take care, not to go out, that you've heard so many things... and you try to stay near her...You hug her again...and

154

make sure that the others in the house are her family. It's warm but you say *It's so cold* and you close the window faster than you mean to . . . Later you leave, reluctantly, shouting *Take caaare!* from the gate. You get home and can't sleep. You're tired from thinking. At last you drop off before you know it. Half an hour later you jump up and let out a scream. You realize it was only a dream. One night goes by like that. The same thing happens the next, but you go back the next day and the next and she's always there. Then one day you find the house closed; the lights are out. You go to the gate and don't hear a sound. You see a broken window shutter, and you see the dog sleeping, but you're not sure it's asleep. You become desperate. You go to the neighbor's for information. When nobody comes out, you swear at yourself. You return to the gate and think that what you were thinking all along has come true, and you want to shout her name with all your strength but you don't dare. You believe they'd cart you off. Then you know what's happened. You feel as if they're strangling you and squat down on a rock. You can't think anymore and just stay there, you stay there to die. Then someone comes down the street and you ask the time. Not till this minute do you notice that all the houses are the same; there's no light in any of them; no dog has barked. You come to your feet, pick up a stone and throw it at the dog you know is dead. As the stone hits him the animal leaps up in a rage, and you're frightened but glad at the same time. And you remember that some kid playing broke the shutter a week ago. A light comes on and a curtain stirs. You smile and curse yourself. You walk backwards slowly, no longer staying there to die. You go away then. You reach home and go to bed. You're bushed. You fall asleep. They wake you up. It's time to go to work. And you say: *What a short night; I've hardly slept at all.* You rise and go.

21

"Do you remember that this is where we talked for the first time? I don't usually come here but I felt so lonely that day," Idalia said to Guillermo.

"Me neither; it was the first time I came in."

"I think you were following me."

"Who knows? Could be. What I remember is that I was on my way to the movies and they were showing *Rambo* to full houses every day."

"Speaking of movies, yesterday *Rambo II* opened."

"So I noticed, but I don't watch that kind of movie anymore: they only make people crazier, and besides you can figure them out. The hero is left all alone because the others chicken out; he does everything alone and always wins."

"Yes, he's all-powerful, can wipe out the whole army of some foreign country."

"It makes me laugh. They're really comedies."

"Uhuh, you've got to bring along your sense of humor when you see them."

"What are you drinking today, beer?"

"Beer. Today I want to drink till I'm drunk."

"Ma'am, two of your coldest beers, please. How come this urge to drink?"

"Well, things."

"For instance?"

"Maybe I'm just happy, or sad, I don't even know."

"Yes you do. Are you going to tell me?"

"Possibly, later on."

"Thanks, Ma'am, and please bring me some change for the juke box. Well okay, but I think you should tell me now."

"Everything in good time. Let me ask you, now that there's no work at the plantation, what do you plan to do?"

"I don't know yet. Look for a job, study, and love you."

"And if I weren't here? What would you do?"

"I don't know, leave here maybe, bum around."

"Sounds nice, and where'd you go?"

"I don't know. Thanks, just a minute, I'm going to play music to put some life into this place. Anything you want to hear?"

"No, thanks. Do you remember what I was listening to the day we met?"

"Yes, but we already knew each other."

"Okay then, the day we talked."

"Yes."

"Uhuh. Listen, has Chago written to you again?"

"Chago, Chago, Chago. No, he never wrote to me."

"I'm serious."

"Me too."

"What about those letters?"

"The letters don't exist; I made them up. I wrote them."

"Be serious, Guillermo."

"Go ahead, laugh. I'm serious; I wrote them. Chago never wrote to me; I never heard from him."

"Really? And why did you do it?"

"What?"

"The letters, the letters, isn't that what we're talking about?"

"Oh, because I always write, besides I wanted to cheer up Chon and Luyi, and the others."

"Have you told them the truth?"

"No, and I'm not going to."

"But if you wrote them, how do you know so much about Tegucigalpa?"

"Oh, people come from there, friends tell me things, then I add a little imagination..."

"You're terrible. Do you still have the letters?"

"Sure."

"I'm sorry but I can't quite believe you. It still seems to me that they're real letters and that Chago actually wrote them."

"It seems that way to me too."

"... funny."

"Sometimes I forget and it seems to me, when I reread the letters, that Chago sent them or at least dictated them to me."

"Only you could dream this up ... Wow, to write letters to yourself."

"I was thirsty. Shall I order you another?"

"If you have the money."

"You're going to make me die laughing."

"It's better to die laughing than any other way."

"Get us two more, please. Something to eat?"

"No, not right now. And you? Aren't you going to have your fried fish today?"

"A little later. I'm going to build up an appetite."

"Lucky you, having to build up an appetite when all around people suffer from chronic hunger."

"So do I. I'm not rich. Only a few days of the year do I allow myself the luxury of saying that."

"Okay, don't get carried away explaining; I was kidding."

"Ding, dong, ding, dong, you can't bargain with love."

"You could become a singer."

"Heck no, but this tune is so catchy. Do you like it?"

"Of course I do; I've already told you."

"Excuse my amnesia."

"You always suffer from it."

"No, only when I'm facing a woman who drives me nuts."

"We'll have to start reserving a place for you in the nut house."

"Like in *The Wall.*"

"Wall? What wall?"

"In the movie."

"Yes, yes, the one with Pink Floyd."

"The guy loses his mind. I'd have liked to see it with you."

"But since we were on the outs, I saw it anyway."

"Did you like it?"

"Of course. The music is beautiful. Besides, it's an anti-fascist movie."

"Yes, very much the thing these days, very pacifist."

"If you go on drinking I'll have to carry you home."

"It's this thirst. I'll order another, aren't you ready yet?"

"No, I'd better take it easy and not get drunk too fast."

"Bring me one, please. They fired Chon."

"Yes, they'll fire everybody."

"What about the Union? Just sitting there with their arms crossed?"

"Who knows. The Union does what it can; I doubt it can do a thing. And since they *disappeared* the president, things just go from bad to worse. There won't be any more Union."

"Chon was crying the day they gave him his walking papers. And he says he won't do piece work."

"So what's he going to do?"

"Fish. Luyi's going to do piece work, even if a lot of people have told him he'll make even less money than before."

"Yes, I'm sure they won't earn enough to eat now."

"That's right, not even enough to eat."

"What are you thinking of so hard now?"

"I was thinking about last night."

"Last night, what happened last night?"

"A crazy dream I had; nothing important."

"I'm sure it's not important, so tell me what it was."

"A silly dream. That they were going to shoot me and were taking me down a long road, a road that stretched for years. One day I got to the place where they were going to shoot me, there was a big crowd waiting. I looked around for somebody whose eyes would say, *Guillermo I'm here and I've come to save you.* But nobody had come for me; they were all just curious. They blindfolded me with a black cloth, tied me to a tree, and then the firing squad positioned itself. I could see through the blindfold: one guy raised his arm as a signal, the men in the squad smiled at one another; instead of guns they carried enormous ballpoint pens, and, obeying orders, they aimed at my chest. The command followed at once and there was a tremendous blast; the men had fired, balls of ink were coming at me in slow motion, growing bigger as they approached, and the men were roaring with laughter because I was so helpless. And I woke up."

"And the great balls of ink didn't hit you?"

"No, I woke up at the exact instant the first drop struck."

"Congratulations, you know how to save yourself from a firing squad."

"More like a ballpoint ink squad."

"Stop making me laugh so much, you're making me spill this."

"It makes no difference how much beer you spill, they won't run out."

"And the money?"

"Nor that either. Ma'am will you let me have a rag for the table; we had an accident."

"The dream was so dreamlike."

"I think you understand."

"What do you think? That you have exclusive rights to the imagination?"

"I didn't say that. The music is over, do you want me to put something else on? Thanks, it's quite clean now, please bring two more beers. Shall I put some music on?"

"Well yes, who doesn't like music? I liked that one very much; I didn't know they had it here."

"Uhuh, *It's your perfume, woman, that always turns me on.* I'm dedicating it to you."

"How nice. Thank you. We have to listen while we can."

"Yes, it's possible that as time goes on they'll ban this kind of music."

"We won't have to wait long; everything coming from Nicaragua will be censored here. They've already started."

"That's right, it is important to travel and get to know places now that they still let you go across. I don't think I'll ever get to go."

"Me neither, but maybe some day. You need a lot of money to travel."

"Right."

"I'll say it again, Guillermo, you ought to become a singer. And, confidentially, you shouldn't sing anymore now; it excites me. It stirs up desires in you too, doesn't it?"

"Yes, in me too. I think we'd better go."

"Did you bring the key?"

"Here it is, and I told my friend not to show up all night."

"You're wicked. Help me get up; I'm very tipsy."

"Miss, the bill please, we're going."

"Hold on to me or I'll fall!"

"With great pleasure precious, I'll never let you go."

"Without squeezing so much."

"Here, keep the change, thanks for everything. We're really going now; it's getting dark."

"Yes, it's getting dark."

22

It was time to be alone, to see one another without being seen, each covering up for the other. In other times he had tried desperately to find the right moment to see her without witnesses, protected by the silent walls and the light-colored ceiling. This way he felt that he alone was her jailer, her kidnapper. And for both, the small world formed by these walls was sufficient for them to tell each other their plans and exchange caresses, to drown themselves in his jokes, or to plot against the world. She happily joined in the search for time to be alone, without people and streets, without trees and rocks, without motors and traffic lights, just the two alone with their words and laughter. In spite of everything, to her Guillermo seemed tender and she needed to see him, to be with him, to love him every day. Several times he tried to break it off, to convince himself that he couldn't fall in love or be sentimentally attached to anyone. He made up his mind to stay clear of the imaginary trap she had set, as if he were a butterfly in a spider's web. And it was all no use because he gradually forgot his outworn macho ideas and glided toward her as if on skis. Nothing could stop it because they needed each other. The room seemed empty, as taut as if the ceiling were about to cave in. And they both had the feeling that this was the last time they'd be trapped by those four walls that had witnessed their beginning and, now, their end. Guillermo had guessed the ending and now wore the look of someone on the edge of an abyss. Idalia would have been lying if she had said that she didn't feel like crying or at least rushing out, running away without being guilty of any crime.

Things had changed so much, too much. And together they had read and reread, word after word, the newspaper account of how the Union president had been found floating in the sea like a boat adrift, his body disfigured with bruises that were the only evidence of the unionist's desperate fight against the vicious sharks that the newspaper heaped curses on. Displayed alongside the story was the picture of an elegant, enormous shark, a species common in that part of the sea. The article warned people against swimming alone, to avoid another tragedy like the Union president's. Let the newspaper reader notice how the unfortunate man's fingernails had been pulled out by the teeth of the monster of the blue waters. And for days people talked about the danger of bathing when the tide was high and no red or green or other color cross was close enough to help. Idalia wasn't talking, because Guillermo looked as if he could see right through her anyway and that checked any desire to talk she may have had. They wanted to tell each other things, to promise *This won't last* and *We'll have time to* . . . Neither of them dared. The situation was very bad in the capital; there was talk of worker and student leaders who disappeared as if by magic and were never heard of again. Newspapers constantly published photographs of unidentified dead persons and complaints about many who were suddenly losing their minds.

Some blamed it on miserable conditions, others on alcohol and drugs, and a public survey said that people were going crazy because of their contempt for Divine Law. Only a few weeks before, Guillermo and Idalia had run into an insane young woman going up and down the main street closing the doors of all the business establishments: the printer's, the drugstore, the pharmacy, the clothing store, the hotel, the movie theater, the café, the bookstore, the pastry shop, the lawyers' offices. And everyone was making a wild dash to reopen the doors of their places of business, as if afraid of being kept prisoner inside. Heads appeared at all the doors to follow with their eyes the madwoman who went on closing doors till she disappeared at the very far end of the avenue. The country was also being overrun by religious sects that contradicted one another in explaining these phenomena. For some it was the last warning that Armageddon was at hand; for others it was only the beginning of horrible sufferings mankind would go through before the Second Coming; others asked people not to listen to theories—not authorized by Holy Scripture—handed out by opposing sects, and so the country was being overrun by everything. Guillermo was sure that this was the product of something new, and, never one to lose his sense of humor, he thought that the purpose of all the military exercises going on in the country in this short time span was to crush the devil's troops that might be getting ready to sabotage God's Judgment Day. Ever since the Union president had disappeared, everything had ended in her country for Idalia. Not that she was afraid or wanted to leave; her going away was an obligation, the fulfillment of a promise to her parents: they had accepted her job with the Union only if in exchange—if things got bad—she'd offer no resistance to going away to Europe to study. She had agreed and she would not defraud them; but her life was staying behind; it was staying because she would spend every second thinking about her return. The president had died and, with him, the Union. The newly formed Union was headed by a worker who drove one of the latest model cars, a pipe smoker who had his fingers in several businesses at the same time. Cigarette smoke filled the whole room. Silent and half-drunk, the two exchanged *looks that could be the last look* as Guillermo recalled from one of his friend's poems.

23

When we make love I feel I'm losing my mind. You shouldn't let yourself get any crazier. Is there anything wrong? No, nothing. News. You have news for me? Good or bad? I don't know. The only thing I want you to know is that I'm tipsy. You know I am too. Yes, I know, but I am more. Have I ever done anything bad to you? No, not at all. Good things are what you've done to me, like a little while ago. Did you like it? Of course I did. You're an animal when you can't hold back anymore. I'm glad I can please you. What about the news? I'll have to start some day, so I'll start now. Aha, so what is it? Well, you know that neither you nor I work at the plantation anymore. Yes, and? Do you remember that the Union president was found dead, and that I was a member of the Union staff? Go on, what then? I have to go on studying and my father, well, you know. Yes, I think I'm catching on: You're leaving? Look, it's my father. Are you leaving? Look. Didn't you hear me? I asked you are you leaving? Let me explain. Are you leaving? Yes, I am. Where to? Abroad, to study. Turn the light on, please. Okay, just a minute, I can't find the switch. My cigarettes, do you remember where I left them? Yes, there, on top of that table. I've got them now. Will you hand me one? With pleasure. You're leaving? Let's talk about something else. About what? About you, what are you going to do? I hadn't decided, but since you're leaving, I'll go too. Where? To the mountain. And there? I have a grandfather; he went away a long time ago. But why go there? I'm going to write; I need solitude. And after that? I don't know, I think once I finish the book I'll go to the capital. To study? Yes, to study and become famous. Funny man, you never lose your sense of humor. One should never lose it. Are you going to dedicate your novel to me? You won't be here, anyway. I'll look for the book when it is published and I'll read it. I hope you like it. If you write the way you make love, who won't like it? I write better. Show-off. It's true. They'll call you arrogant. For something that's true. Maybe by then there'll be pills for ego trips. It's possible; once Chago gave me a pill for the heat. Is it really true he didn't write to you? No, people go away and you never hear anything again from any of them. Not all of them. You'll see when you're gone; you won't know who we are anymore. I won't forget you, any of you. You'd better not. Is that a threat? I guess so. What I regret is that we made so little love when we had so much time. You'd better believe it. Me too, who wouldn't?

Guillermo stubbed the cigarette butt out in the ashtray and lit another. They looked at each other. He was pacing the floor. She watched him from the bed, sitting there, smoking slowly. He let out a guffaw.

What's the matter, have you gone crazy? No, you and I are crazy. Why? We shouldn't waste the little time we have left locked up in here. We have to have a going-away party. And what do you suggest? We already made love. We can go dancing, get drunk, wish each other luck, and come back here to say goodbye. Really? Of course. You amaze me; you're unique. Get dressed fast, because I'm just about ready to attack you. Don't laugh so loud, you'll scare the neighbors. Long live laughter! Get dressed. Naturally, my sweet little thing, dressed is the word. This will be a real goodbye. First I want to ask you a question. Go ahead, shoot. Do you love me? Of course I do, and you me? Ditto. Then, Idalia, if we love each other who's to blame for separating us? I don't know, Guillermo, I believe Standard is.

24

The propellers raised a hurricane of dust mixed with dry leaves and newspapers forgotten in the streets. The steady tup tup tup of the two hundred helicopters revving up at the same time was deafening for kilometers around and, unwillingly, the hearts of the townspeople, not to mention those just passing through, followed the tup tup tup of the engines with each beat in their terrified chests. Some time back, in other parts of the country, similar things had taken place. Not long before, American troops in a joint effort with Honduran troops had invaded the port of Trujillo where, because of a misleading report, the ambassador had been trapped in the cross fire. When he tried to escape in his airplane it was too late: paratroopers were descending through the sky and aircraft were strafing the zones where the enemy supposedly lay in wait. For a few seconds the ambassador ran in circles on the runway, yelling his head off in English and trying to pick up his glasses which had been sent flying. Combat troops shouted at him simultaneously in two languages to get out of where his life was a target both for his allies and for enemy troops that kept up tremendous bomb explosions and sustained bursts of gunfire. Several soldiers exposed themselves going to rescue the ambassador; he had lost his glasses for the third time and was stumbling about as if in a nightmare. The ambassador was rescued and immediately taken to an armored hangar with an excellent lookout from where he watched every movement of the U.S. and Honduran troops allied to defeat an invisible enemy moving with the agility only an invisible army could possess. When the fighting ended in that sector, the ambassador mopped his sweaty face with a handkerchief and said: "We couldn't get away in time, but we had the best seats in the house." Then he caught sight of his glasses resting on the ground, smashed into millions of particles.

A few months before, these same troops had invaded an area near the Nicaraguan border. And now military exercises were planned for the invasion of La Ceiba. The entire city had been waiting tensely ever since news bulletins had announced that at any moment there would be thousands of combined American and Honduran troops taking La Ceiba. Guillermo, whose home was close to the Air Force base, had never dreamed that things could take such a disastrous turn. In every corner of the city people ran into Americans who, while still some distance off, identified themselves as soldiers. In the past La Ceibans had grown accustomed to foreign visitors but they had not been like these. In their front yards, older men were talking about how different the gringos who had visited the country when they were young had been. They spoke about nice Americans in washed-out blue jeans and checkered shirts, Americans with shoulder-length hair and knapsacks, who introduced them to rock, Americans without uniforms or guns, who didn't get drunk and beat up the natives, Americans who didn't play around with Honduran girls and get them pregnant, Americans who came with money and paid for the local people sitting next to them, Americans who didn't bring contagious deadly venereal diseases and didn't run down students coming out of the University in Jeeps, Americans like the writer O. Henry, Americans who didn't come here to give orders to decent Honduran soldiers or train them to kill, Americans who learned to love the Honduran people and would sit in the moonlight with their guitars and play music that nobody understood but everybody liked, Americans who when it was time to leave town turned so sad they seemed to be grieving.

The people were absolutely terrified now and what made it worse was that a few weeks before, during carnival festivities, four fighter planes had broken the sound barrier at the same time; two hundred thousand people who had collected in the main avenue to dance along its entire length started running, in panic, scared out of their wits, with the kind of horror they had only felt at the movies, watching films about the war in Vietnam. In many buildings store windows or walls came crashing down, and the frenzy of the crowds, driven berserk by the powerful jet blasts, caused more damage. Several children were lost or trampled by unfeeling shoes that seemed to be motorized; many women went out into the street stark naked; men shouted the names of their children and their wives in the middle of the human stampede. From every mouth you could hear *War is here I knew there was going to be a war The newspapers talked about the war Listen everyone Go home War against Nicaragua War The Sandinistas have come to eat children and steal cows Run for your lives They're here to destroy the country.* And the screams of wounded children and women crying in pain, and then in the midst of the excited crush of people anti-riot soldiers appeared with megaphones asking people to calm down and explaining at the top of their voices that there was nothing wrong that it was just an experiment to liven up the carnival for the parton saint San Isidro, that the enemy couldn't come in so easily because we're prepared to wipe them out, *So take it easy Nothing's wrong You must have faith in us and in God Have faith that we are invincible*. And La Ceiba never forgot that although the carnival had continued it had been ruined, for there were wakes in many homes and the hospital wasn't big enough for all the wounded.

The rumor that the city would be invaded in the next few hours had everybody worried. Helicopters kept up their tup tup tup, suddenly taking off in groups, and all over the city paratroopers started dropping from the skies. Airplanes and tanks and bursts of machine-gun fire; thousands of Honduran and foreign soldiers scurrying zigzag all over the place. The helicopters continued to take off or land and the hearts of the civilian population were beating in their chests as desperately as when someone being hunted down starts pounding on the door. From some of the houses, among them Guillermo's, the zinc sheets of the roofs began to fly off and the walls softened and collapsed under the tup tup tup of the motors blowing down trees and sheets of zinc on top of the pot of beef soup on top of the typewriter on top of the furniture just recently paid for. And Guillermo's mother screaming to her other children *Run Saul Get out of the house Run Saul That post is about to fall on top of you Watch out Karlaaa* and the tup tup tup scaring the little girl who runs screaming without shoes or any clothes on looking for mama and *Mama Fernando is missing Help me get Fernaaando out* and the tup tup tup beating on those walls that managed to stay up, trembling as if there was an earthquake and their mother screaming *Stop those goddam things you fuckin' gringos* and the tup tup tup swallowing her words and she's crying with her children around her watching her house come down and Guillermo her oldest far away working where it also reaches him but not as loud the tup tup tup of the two hundred and it's not till many hours later that everything quiets down again and there are no paratroopers in the sky but the ears of the civilian population are still ringing tup tup tup. And it's late and Guillermo comes home, hugs his mother and asks no questions because he doesn't know what to ask. And an eery silence falls over everything. The maneuvers are over. It's been announced that the military exercises are moving to another part of the country tup tup tup.

25

That same day, after the helicopters had gone, Guillermo began to rebuild his home with the help of the neighbors, who joined in one by one. The sound of hammers started up everywhere, and you could hear sheets of zinc being dragged from place to place and the shouts of neighbors *Grab that board Marcos and set it straight. Pass me the saw, Maria. Get me a glass of water Javiercito. Did all the plates break? Marquitos get out of the way dammit a plank's ready to fall on you. Go home. They didn't break, the troops broke them, which is a different story. Guillermo, have you got any more nails there? Yes, yes, just a minute.*

Union is strength and there's nowhere to turn, that's how it is. Hurry. We're getting somewhere with these repairs. This takes balls. We're fucked, all shot to hell; where can we go put in a complaint? Who can we tell that my mother's house fell down? We sink lower every day, we sink into the profound depths of Honduras and we sit on our hands, forgetting everything and—as if we were blind—that they do things right in our faces and we don't look. (Here are the nails don Carlos.)

This is going from bad to worse. What good are maneuvers? They're good for war. It's war right in front of our homes and we say nothing. It's someone else's war dropped on us from the clouds. War starts with chopping up the air to destroy our houses. What have they fed us Hondurans to make us deaf, dumb, blind, and not able to smell gunpowder or blood right in front of our faces? What will become of us? Where are we headed? (Pass me the hammer please, don Miguel.) *We have to work in all things like we're doing right now. United. We have to look for that lost unity. We're sinking and no one helps us hold our heads above water. We must be the ones to do it, alone, because even the Bible says help yourself and I will help you and we don't help one another. We're like robots whose heads nod that everything's fine, yes whatever you say, there's no problem, yes it's all right. It's sad my mother's crying but your house is going up mom. Look at the way we're all pitching in to put it up again. Look at how the whole neighborhood has come around. Look mom, we're the whole barrio, after all we're the people and we're never wrong, we're like ants, indestructible, and we never give up.*

And to show twice as much contempt for the Law we did our thinking in a place where there was plenty of peace. And I looked for shelter in the clouds, in the center of the earth, in the ocean depths, and I couldn't find it. Peace—I thought—was in flight into the country itself, into my own country. It was huddled in some corner, waiting for someone to come to its rescue. Now Beti looks at me again; she's serious this time. Is war crossing her mind? But no, Beti can't be wasting her time thinking about war, since it's the only thing that hasn't been banned. Anyone can think about war, even the biggest fool. The authorities hand out tickets, lots of them, by the dozen or any way you want them, to think about war. Beti is with me here to think of what you can't think about outside of this place: about peace, about escaping, the family, the neighbors, the government, the Law, about doing things, conspiring, about to-morrow, the sun, solidarity, friends, etcetera. And Beti—with eyes caught between fear and astonishment—is doing nothing but thinking about the damn war. I feel like telling her to stop thinking about it. We have to stick to our agreement: not a word inside the cave. And now Beti is looking at me with horror in her eyes, envisioning gunpow-der, bombs, missiles. And I'm nervous, *Please don't Beti, You'd better think of peace* I am thinking. Beti shakes her head, she has understood me, she lowers her eyes and smiles nervously. And she asks me with her eyes if I sense something strange, if I hear noises. And I'm shaking my head to say no. I keep on telling her no. I want to tell her that the approaching shadows are not uniformed soldiers with guns trained on us, are nothing but the fruit of this beautiful crime: thinking.

THE END

—GUILLERMO LÓPEZ LÓPEZ

—*April, some corner in Central America.*

26

They had spent all day together, covering the city from end to end. And they had had a lot to say to each other but had walked in silence most of the time. Chon and Luyi had found out that Guillermo was going away the next day and had traveled from El Porvenir to meet with him and say goodbye. They asked few questions. He told them about the trouble with his house, how it had crashed to the ground and how all the neighbors had pitched in to raise it up again. Chon had looked at the sky, saying, "It would've been better if man had never learned to fly." And Luyi had also looked up and visored a hand over his eyes without saying a word. They talked about war as something far off but inevitable. Chon told them about his new plans, and more than once remembered some joke that for the time being took their minds off the sadness of goodbyes. Guillermo thought of the letters that Chago had never written and was about to let them know the truth when Chon brought up Chago's name to say "He should be here; or maybe not. Maybe he's living very well these days." Luyi made no bones about how happy he was that he had moved to El Porvenir and mentioned several times how fond he was becoming of Chon's kids. Guillermo thought about his mother, the house they had rebuilt, the tup tup tup of the helicopters and then of Chon's kids as the alternative for a better future. He thought of Chon's kids and then said what he was thinking out loud: "They're the children of El Porvenir, the children of the Future." Chon and Luyi asked for an explanation, so Guillermo smiled and apologized for going around thinking out loud. They had wandered from place to place for many hours, but now the evening was being cut short by the old men's concern that they might not be able to catch a bus. Guillermo suggested that their farewell walk end at the beach. And Chon couldn't hide the feelings this idea stirred in him, feelings aroused in him whenever he heard anyone mention the sea.

27

This is where everything ends, Chon had said. And both Guillermo and Luyi seemed to confirm it with their silence. Under the clear sky for a few minutes they were like statues in front of the sea, the breeze making them squint and also providing them with an excuse to keep from looking directly at one another. Luyi sat down on the sand and the others followed his lead. *So you're going to your grandfather's place to write; I hope everything turns out good for you,* he heard Chon's voice and to Guillermo the voice, carried on the wind, seemed to come out of the far side of the sea. *That's right,* he answered, after a pause that said much more than his words. Crestfallen, Luyi said, *We'll see one another again some day,* without any conviction, and repeated the same thing again without realizing it. The cigarettes in Luyi's and Guillermo's lips and the tobacco in Chon's back teeth halted the conversation. The waves beating the shore seemed to be trying to climb out of the water, and Luyi's eyes, sadder than usual, were riveted on them as if to tell them there was nothing he could do to set them free. *The way those guys walk is familiar to me,* Chon remarked without taking his eyes off the two men heading in their direction. *To me too,* Luyi said, overjoyed. *It's them,* Guillermo yelled and the three scrambled to their feet and went to meet the new arrivals: exchange of greetings, fast jokes, and spontaneous opinions, *You've put on so much weight, You never get older, We've come to take a ship because we're going to Haiti, I never thought I'd see you two again, Lucifer has no power to separate hearts that love one another, You're already sprouting a mustache,* and laughter on all their faces. The five men sat down in a circle, like in the old days; there were backslaps and friendly elbow jabs. *Incredible* became the word of the hour, passing from one mouth to the next. Lelo and Fabian emptied the bags they carried and passed out bread, candy, fruits. *What are you doing here?* Fabian asked. And Luyi's voice sounded full of enthusiasm: *Visiting the sea.* Lelo bit into a piece of candy, raised one hand and pointed with his index finger: *The sea is one of the most marvelous and sacred of God's divine works; you do right to visit it.* Guillermo remembered the day they had been to the beaches in El Porvenir and Lelo had not wanted to go in the water because it was so easy for Lucifer to enter the sea. *Things are all fucked up here, everything tells us that we're going to starve to death,* Chon said. Fabian spoke, with long pauses between his words, *Nobody starves to death as long as he follows the good path, waters the land and earns his bread with the sweat of his brow.* Luyi let out a horselaugh: *You can't tell anymore if it's Lelo or Fabian talking; they're exactly alike, identical in everything.* Chon came out with one of his usual jokes: *Lelo's a rascal; who knows what he's been doing to Fabian in his sleep; have you ever woke up with your pants pulled down to your knees?* Fabian was furious: *Only he who walks among the wicked knows wickedness by heart.* Lelo, the teacher talking to his misguided student, told him: *Fabian, patience is a sign that a man has found peace; laughter and jokes are for those who have become like brothers; humor exists only in loyal and special hearts.* Fabian bowed his head as if he were vowing never to forget the lesson. Guillermo was thinking of Idalia; he wasn't sad. He felt that few persons could be as understanding as he was, as capable of accepting whatever happened. The only thing that made him feel bad was that Idalia hadn't read a line of his short story. He wished he had read it to her, to show her how hard he was trying, to let her know that she was Beti, she alone, because Beti was real. He was sorry he hadn't explained that he had written the story with the two of them in mind, dreaming that one day in the future this would be how they would be. He remembered the poet, the day of their beers and their goodbye; it had stayed in his memory, like a recording, when he told him: *Guillermo, my colleague, keep plugging away, you've got everything in your favor to make you go far. We'll meet one day in some writers' conference, okay?* And Guillermo had sworn that they would. Now he wondered if what the poet had told him was true or if it had only been the beers or the sadness speaking, brought on by his having to go away. He consoled himself with the thought that they really hadn't had so much to drink, that the poet wasn't unsteady on his feet, that if he had stumbled it was because the floor had been wet and it was more than likely that the poet's shoes slipped easily. A black teenager carrying a sack came over to the group: *Would you like some coconut milk?* Lelo stood up, *I'll treat, we must drink coconut water, it brings good luck, it cleans out your conscience.* The black lowered his sack and started cutting a hole in each coconut with a machete. Luyi, who was looking at the sea, let out a happy shout: *The ships are coming, the ships are coming.* And those sitting down got up and they all stood facing the sea, with their backs to La Ceiba. Luyi was pointing and repeating: *The ships are coming, the ships are back.* Chon watched him sadly and said: *It's not the same as before, there's no use in the ships coming, there's no more extra work hours; besides, they pay very little and you're the only one working at the plantation, Luyi.* Luyi's cheerful mood disappeared completely. Lelo looked at the grey ships and said: *Those ships are not the ships of the good, they are Lucifer's, they're war ships; that's why they're such a dark color, like the darkness of Hell.*

Looking at Lelo, Guillermo remembered the news on the radio and in the papers that said there would be war against Nicaragua because the Sandinistas wanted to invade, and he thought about everything: Idalia, Chago, the foreign troops, his short story, a better future, the poet, the plantation.

"The ships of death are coming," Chon said and Guillermo was still thinking about peace, music, Chon's kids, a new world without Firsts or Thirds, and about his grandfather holed up in the mountains.

"The ships of Judgment Day," Fabian contradicted.

And Guillermo's mind went on remembering his mother, the rain, the yellowbeards, the lunch hour, the Red Book, El Porvenir.

"Lucifer's ships," Lelo muttered.

And Guillermo's brain seemed untiring: the beach, Idalia's mother, the strike, the railway, pay day, the letters Chago had never written to him, the helicopters.

"Those ships aren't like the ones before, like the white ships," Luyi called out.

And Guillermo was thinking about the ships and his novel and without taking his eyes off the sea, he sighed:

"The ships, the ships after all, the same ships as always, with one difference, they have changed color."